## FIRE FROM HEAVEN

The first five charges detonated all at once, blowing rock and dust over the camp. The rebel soldiers stopped what they were doing and stared up at the cliff that loomed over them.

Five more explosions occurred.

Then there was a pause, but in the pause came a rumble, and as the rebels watched with horrified fascination, a slice of the cliff came loose and began sliding directly toward the camp.

The third set of Applebaum's explosions was triggered. The wedge broke apart, and a third of a million tons of debris rained down on the Communist encampment.

Marty sat in the Toyota with the board in his lap. "I hate it, I just hate it, Harry, when I don't get to watch."

# THE DEATH MACHINE CONTRACT

## BOOKS BY MICHAEL MCDOWELL AND JOHN PRESTON

THE BLACK BERETS

*Deadly Reunion*
*Cold Vengeance*
*The Black Palm*
*Contract: White Lady*
*Louisiana Firestorm*
*The Death Machine Contract*
*The Red Man Contract*
*D.C. Death March*
*The Night of the Jaguar*
*Contract: Terror Summit*
*The Samurai Contract*
*The Akbar Contract*
*Blue Water Contract*

# THE DEATH MACHINE CONTRACT

MICHAEL MCDOWELL
& JOHN PRESTON

BLACK
STONE
PUBLISHING

Published in 2023 by Blackstone Publishing
Cover design by Bookfly Design
Book design by Blackstone Publishing



Printed in the United States of America

ISBN 979-8-200-88196-3
Fiction / War & Military

Version 1

Blackstone Publishing
31 Mistletoe Rd.
Ashland, OR 97520

www.BlackstonePublishing.com

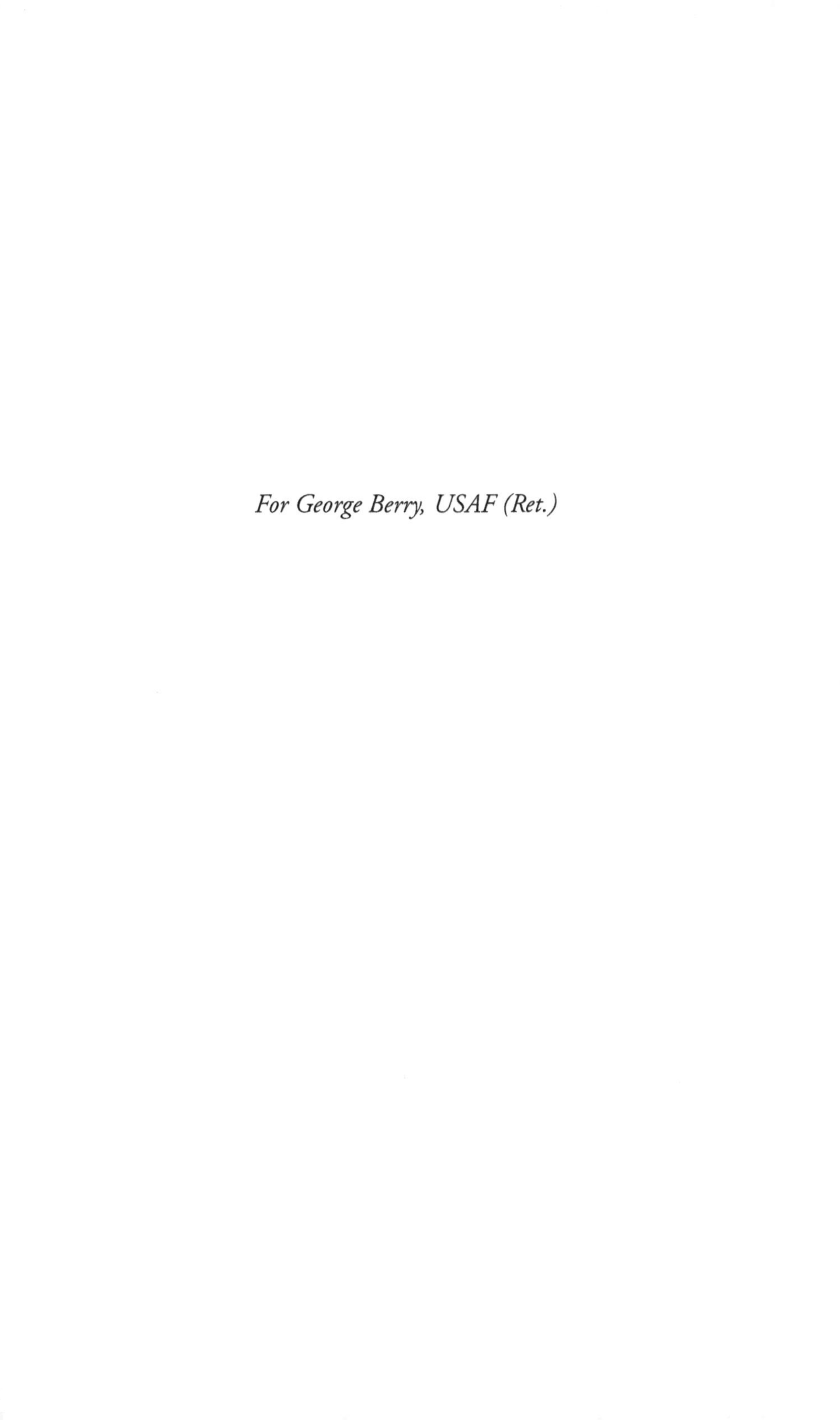

*For George Berry, USAF (Ret.)*

# 1

He knew that the stewardess thought he was some kind of high roller. He just sighed. That made sense. Sure it did. Here he was on a flight to Las Vegas and his ticket reservation had clearly read *Harry the Greek*. He didn't really like the implication that he was trying to be some kind of obnoxious big shot, but he was just damned tired of going around spelling his impossible name to every high-school-dropout ticket agent in the country.

Even when they got it right, it never fit on the ticket, or on the airline's computer forms. Haralambos Georgeos Pappathanassiou just wasn't a handle you ran off in a quick and easy phone conversation to make airline reservations. If he had to stop and spell the damn thing every time he got on a plane he would never have been able to leave Chicago in the first place.

Maybe that wouldn't have been such a bad idea, never to have left Chicago.

Harry looked out the window of the 727 and watched the small terminal building of Shreveport Airport as it diminished in the shimmering distance. The plane was winding over the maze of runways, taxiing into place for takeoff.

What would life have been like, he wondered, if none of it had begun?

If he hadn't gone to Vietnam?

If he had refused to join the SEALs, the navy's most elite fighting force?

If he hadn't met Marty once he was in?

Or, once he'd returned from Vietnam, what would life have been like if he'd stayed in Chicago? Just kept his bar and downed his bottle of Scotch every night in the dimly lighted rooms on the second floor?

What if Billy Leaps Beeker hadn't found him and brought him back?

What if the Black Berets hadn't regrouped?

As long as he was at it, he asked himself: What if I had never been born?

Because the way that Harry figured it, once he had been born, everything else was inevitable.

Pretty miserable, but inevitable.

At any point in his life, if he had made a choice different from the one he actually did make, then it wouldn't matter. He'd still end up in the same place, right there, in the first-class section of a 727, taxiing up to a sticky runway in Louisiana, on his way to Las Vegas.

With Marty Applebaum beside him.

And no matter what different choices Harry would have made in his life, there'd be Marty, saying just what he was saying now. "Hey, Harry, man, this is gonna be hot shit. I mean, this is gonna be the best vacation in the whole goddamn world, and all the rest of those guys can sit at home and pick their noses for all I care."

The plane was in position. The engines began to rev up. The pilot moved the plane forward, steadily increasing the ground speed until the sharp lift-up told Harry they were airborne.

On their way to Las Vegas, a city that Harry hated less than he hated most other cities.

Marty was leaning across Harry to stare out the window. He always did this. Took the aisle seat, so that the adolescent in him could goose the stewardesses. But leaned across Harry because the even smaller boy in him wanted to look out the window.

Marty seemed so small—small as that little boy in him sometimes.

Next to Harry, of course, most people looked pretty small. The Greek was six two and weighed two twenty. He figured that because he'd been in training with the team for over a year now and had gone on five assignments with them, he was in such top shape he might have qualified as a weightlifter. If he had cared about trying.

He didn't.

He didn't care about much.

Marty. He guess he cared about Marty. Probably because nobody else did. Marty didn't make a wonderful first impression. He was thin and spindly. His blond hair was so thin it gave you the idea he'd been losing it forever. Always going, going, it was never quite gone. His breathing was often tortured, the result of a childhood bout of asthma that he'd concealed from the Army. As much time as Marty spent outdoors, he was pale. If exposed to the sun for more than a couple of hours he'd develop a lobster-red sunburn. But the skin bleached out overnight, and peeled, and he was as pale as ever.

Marty didn't improve on closer acquaintance, either. Beneath that unsightly exterior, there didn't lurk a truly wonderful human being.

"Harry, the red-headed stewardess, I just know she wants me to pork her. Harry, soon as this bird gets going, I'm gonna get her in one of those little bathrooms and give it to her. She'll have her panties off so quick her thighs'll get windburn. She's waiting. She wants me. I can tell."

Harry nodded. It was the only way to deal with Marty's constant bragging. Just nod. Harry never questioned Marty's claims. Sure, the shit about women was shit. Harry had never so much as seen Marty leave a room with a woman, and the only proof of Marty's prowess was—as they said in court—hearsay. And it was Marty's own. But if it made him feel better, what the hell? Let him rattle.

The weird thing was, the rest of Marty's bragging was real. Soon, probably within fifteen minutes after takeoff, when he got a drink in his hand, Marty would start another line of bravado, but this one would be real. About battles and explosions he'd triggered, the men he'd killed. No exaggeration there. And Marty didn't have to go very far back in his memory to fetch these stories up. Didn't have to go back to Vietnam. Marty could tell stories about last week.

Marty loved bombs. Just loved them. In a way, he made love *to* them. Sometimes elegantly, the way he had offed that group of Indonesian terrorists with a synchronized, color-coordinated demolition show. Sometimes—when he hadn't time for preparation—just quickly and efficiently. But Marty didn't like this "sloppy" work. Where was the pleasure of blasting an oil storage facility with a grenade launcher? All you got was one massive, uncontrolled explosion.

Style. That's what Marty brought to the Black Berets' explosive capabilities. Made death pretty. Gave it form and balance.

But off the field, Marty just had no control. He was loud, boisterous, never figured out the right thing to say, but never had any problem finding the wrong one.

And the rest of them . . .

There were five Black Berets. Marty and Harry were taking a vacation in Las Vegas, leaving the other three back on the farm, Billy Leaps Beeker's farm outside of Shreveport.

The farm was like some sort of voracious amoeba, constantly shooting out in various directions, gobbling up more land, growing larger and more peculiarly shaped by the month. As soon as any land contiguous to the property came up for sale, Billy Leaps bought it. Sometimes the rest of them thought that the half-breed Cherokee was trying to buy back the whole county from the Anglos, as though his accumulation of property deeds would repurchase the pride of the Indian people.

How much was there now? Over five hundred acres? Harry had lost track. Six hundred forty was the magic number—a square mile of property. But of course once he'd achieved that, Beeker just started work on the second square mile. He'd even started, just recently, to buy land that wasn't contiguous to his own holdings. "Sometime," he'd said, "I'll get the land that lies between . . . ."

The man made a fetish of his real estate. That, and his son. Tsali. A seventeen-year-old purebred Cherokee, mute, the product of countless foster homes and juvenile centers. Beeker had saved him from torture and ignominious death at the hands of two redneck farmers. At that moment, with all the depth that could ever be established between a boy and a man, Tsali had become Beeker's son.

The formal adoption came later. But those papers and the will in which Beeker left everything to the boy weren't really necessary. The mute kid lived for the big scarred marine. Billy Leaps had lost part of an ear at Khe Sanh. It was something important for everyone to remember: a physical manifestation of what he had lost in his soul in Vietnam. Tsali was compensation for that.

Beeker had married twice. He hadn't particularly liked the

women—Harry knew that. He had hated living with them. The demands of suburban domesticity had been utterly alien to him. But he'd gone through with the charade for a single reason—to father a son. It hadn't happened, not with either of the wives. When it had become clear that he wasn't to get a son that way, he'd given up hope.

*Hopeless*. Harry thought about that. Maybe Harry hadn't plumbed the depths—at least not the way Billy Leaps Beeker had. Because at least when Beeker submerged himself into that true hopelessness, he'd managed to come back again. Like a diver who dives deep, deeper, deepest, but shoots back up when he hits bottom. He found Tsali, and he regrouped the Black Berets—almost simultaneously.

But nothing as good as that was going to happen to Harry. He was just diving through water that didn't have a bottom.

If he fought against himself harder, maybe he'd end up like Cowboy, one of the other Black Berets. Cowboy was a pilot. Always had been. His daddy had been one of the original barnstormers, living for no reason other than the privilege of flying planes. Didn't matter for what reason. He'd put on daredevil shows for the county fair, spray crops, run contraband, fly geologists and mappers—anything that would put fuel in his gas tanks was a reason for Cowboy's daddy to live.

Cowboy inherited all of that, and a little more too.

By the time it was his turn to learn how to take a plane up, jets were the thing, the sound barrier had been broken, and missiles were just a little way down the line. You had to go to college and learn science and engineering and God only knew what else to get certified. So Cowboy had hauled his ass off to Texas A&M and done it all.

Cowboy, the barnstormer's son, had walked out of that place with more than a pilot's license. He had a computer whiz's knowledge of electronics. He hadn't gone after it. It had dropped on his head. Cowboy's prowess in this was apparent in the Louisiana farm's security system. Strictly state-of-the-art. A legless dog crawling with his head down couldn't have gotten five feet inside the perimeter of the farm without seventeen alarms going on, all of them screaming, *Look out for the legless dog! He's coming this way!*

As good as Cowboy was with all that technological stuff, he was better with cocaine. Harry thought that might be the answer. If he couldn't embrace nothingness the way Beeker had, maybe he should try heavy drugs.

Mother C, Cowboy called it. The lady whose love you could count on. Beeker hated the crap. He had forbade any of them to use drugs while they were in the field—or while they were training to be in the field. Their leader had a warrior ethic that demanded full consciousness and total commitment to the mission. Cowboy could bitch and scream for the rest of his life, but the truth was, no cocaine while Beeker was in charge. Like all the rest of them, Cowboy had submitted. Not with what you'd call a good grace, but he hadn't finally challenged Beeker's authority. None of them had. Not in any way.

They had lived for years after Vietnam without the military discipline that had given their lives structure. Without that sustaining pin, their lives had fallen apart. Cowboy had become a smuggler, taking his pay in white powder that he took out of Colombia and dropped off in Texas. Harry had run his bar during the day and guzzled his stock at night. Marty had taken a job with a demolition company, always pretending that a dozen gooks were hiding in every room of the empty hotels he was blowing up. And Rosie . . .

The huge black man was the last of the Black Berets to float through Harry's mind. He closed his eyes at the image of

Rosie when they'd found him again, ten years after Vietnam. In the basement of Newark City Hospital. In the morgue, with a sharp knife, peeling the skin off cadavers to make bandages for burn victims. Rosie stayed sane after Vietnam by carrying on conversations with dead people while he stripped off their skin.

They had been adrift, all of them, until that week when Beeker went around the country and told them, "It's time. We're going back."

Their first mission had been a scam. But they'd turned it around. Because they were a team now. The Black Berets, a small, skilled, ferocious group of men. Maybe there were others somewhere in the world that were smaller, more skilled, and meaner—but Harry doubted it. Hard to put together five men who could do as much damage as they could, even in a world with four billion human beings in it.

Lots of people knew it. Too many. The team was getting a reputation. When five guys can bring down a government, exterminate a city of terrorists, lay waste to a whole sect of fanaticism, then word gets around.

Harry and Marty had earned this vacation—every second of it—on mission after mission. Earned it with hot sweat and hard labor. They were in peak shape, they were as well trained as they came, and they had the best leader they would ever find on this earth: Billy Leaps Beeker.

They had come back to the team, and the team meant Beak. The half-breed Cherokee who said that a warrior's life was the definition of honor, that battle was his destiny, and that his reward was a calmness of soul and a quick death.

They all hated him just a little, they all respected him a whole lot, and each one of them loved him in some private corner of his soul. You had to. He held your life in his hand. You went where he told you to go. You did what he commanded.

He had given their lives structure and meaning again. Without him and what he had done for them, they were nothing.

Now they were warriors.

Each of them a time bomb. Ticking away as they strolled the Shreveport malls, peering in the windows. Ticking away as they turned restlessly in their beds with old nightmares. Ticking away as they simply sat in the first-class section of a 727 five miles up over Kansas.

It was Billy Leaps who controlled the timer on the bombs that were named Harry, Marty, Cowboy, and Rosie.

But who controlled the timer on the bomb that was called Beeker?

Harry had thought about that a lot. Billy Leaps must be a lonely man—that's why he was so close to Tsali. No one above him, no general. He should have had a general to direct him. A general to plan strategy. A general was a god, to whom questions of morality and long-term consequence were directed. But Beeker didn't have a general.

He just had Delilah.

Delilah was from Washington, and the lady knew things.

The lady was gorgeous, and the lady sometimes occupied Beeker's bed, and the lady gave them maps and said, "There's some trouble at the spot marked *X*."

The Black Berets didn't know whom Delilah worked for. Could have been anybody. Could have been for her own damn pleasure. They couldn't be sure.

But she hadn't steered them wrong yet.

And any woman who could handle Beeker . . .

"She's dripping," said Marty in a low, intense voice, staring at the stewardess. "I can *smell* how much she wants it . . . ."

The stewardess, who to Harry's eye looked pretty dry, asked if Harry and Marty would like anything to drink.

Marty grinned at her. "Yeah, I'll take a screwdriver."

Harry shook his head. It was before lunch. He didn't want anything.

He looked at the stewardess. Pretty. Plastic smile. But what else could she do? If Harry had to smile, his smile would look faker than hers—he was sure of that. And the lady didn't deserve what Marty said about her either. She looked like a good girl. Probably got a nice family, maybe a boyfriend on the side, one of the pilots up front. House in the suburbs somewhere, couple of kids, lawn that got mowed every other week in the summer, and not a single gun in the house. What would it have been like to have led a normal life like that, Harry wondered, with a wife who was an airline stewardess, and two kids in public school, and—

He sat up straight. Very straight. Frozen in position.

The motion caught Marty's attention.

"What is it?" he said quickly, looking from Harry back over to the stewardess. She'd been leaning over to take the orders of a group of three men sitting on the other side of the first-class cabin from Harry and Marty.

Hispanics. Mid-twenties. Sharply dressed. Quiet. Cool.

Since the flight had taken off they'd been talking quietly together. Just whispers. A little vague, even nervous laughter. The kind of laughter you hear out of someone who's flying for the first time.

Or hijacking a plane for the first time.

The stewardess stood up and Harry could see that her face was pale with fear. Very professionally, she walked to the front of the plane and disappeared into the cockpit. She returned after a few moments with the copilot. His face too was gripped with concern. He stood in front of the three Hispanics and Harry could see his jaw tremble with anger.

"Gentlemen," he said with controlled politeness.

The man closest to him stood up and smiled in his face. "Ladies and gentlemen," he said to those in the first-class compartment, "*viva Castro.*"

# 2

"Ah shit, Harry, they're not!" cried Marty in disgust.

Harry put a restraining hand on the little man's arm, but Marty had already lost it. "They are *not* gonna hijack this fucking plane to Cuba, are they? I am on my way to Las Vegas for my vacation and a thousand whores, I am not gonna waste my time on some goddamn commie island in the middle of the goddamn ocean. I want the goddamn desert!"

"Marty . . ." Harry started to speak in his usual calm voice, but the copilot had returned to the cockpit and now was employing the intercom system to inform the passengers of the slight change in flight plans.

"Ladies and gentlemen, we're sorry to have to tell you that this flight is being forcibly rerouted to Havana. There is no need for alarm. We—"

A shrill scream of panic roared out from the tourist section behind the heavy curtains and drowned out the copilot's further words. The stewardesses rushed back to help stem the furor.

"I can't fucking believe this," said Marty, crossing his arms tightly across his narrow chest and pushing back his seat as far as it would go. "I can't fucking believe it."

In a few moments the roar died down, and the only sound to be heard was a murmur of convulsive sobbing. Things were better in the first-class cabin, where every passenger sat still and silent and calm, and no one even looked back at the hijackers in the cabin with them.

The copilot came on again. "Procedures for emergencies of this sort have their own protocol, ladies and gentlemen. We will land in Havana and be back in the sky in less than a day. We will return to Shreveport and then—"

"*A day!* That's it, Harry. I'm not putting up with this shit. A day that I could be at poolside with women in both hands. And we're going back to Shreveport first? That'd be *two* days out of a five-day vacation. I'm gonna miss two days at the tables? No way, Harry, no way."

"I'll take 'em out," Harry said quietly.

"Hell you will!" Marty jerked his head around and stared in Harry's calm face. His own was flushed and twitching. "*The hell you will.* This is my vacation they're screwing up. I'm going to handle it."

"My vacation too," said Harry.

"Yeah," said Marty, with a wicked twinkle in his eye, "but I'm on the aisle. That means it's mine."

"I think I ought to handle it," said Harry.

"Are you saying I can't?"

*Damn.* Harry had done it again. Put Marty in the situation where he thinks he's being put down. No way to make him stay still after that. He'd take the words as an insult and *insist* on dealing with the hijackers himself. Harry knew better than try to use reasoning or logic.

"Let's flip for it," he suggested.

While Marty was digging in his pocket for a couple of coins, one of the Hispanic hijackers came back and passed out several leaflets of pro-Communist, pro-Castro literature.

Harry took it and said, "Thanks."

"Match, you go," said Marty, handing Harry a quarter. "No match, I go."

The two coins were flipped into the air. Each man caught his and slapped it down on the back of his hand.

Harry uncovered his first. "Heads."

Marty peeked at his before uncovering, grinned a broad grin, and said, "Tails."

"Let me see it," said Harry. Marty cheated sometimes.

"You don't trust me?"

"Nope."

Marty uncovered the coin. It was tails. Marty bounced up and down in his seat with glee. He'd not only won the toss, he'd put one over on Harry as well. "Goddamn, you thought I was cheating!" He cackled so loudly that everyone in the cabin turned to stare at him.

"Fine," said Harry, "it's yours."

It wasn't that Harry didn't think Marty could do it. But the little man always carried things too far. He was always taking chances that weren't necessary if he thought it would make him look better before whatever audience he had.

Harry would have just done it. Just taken them out. Marty was going to make a production of it.

The Greek reached into the seat pocket, took out the pro-Communist pamphlet, and opened it up. It was written in execrable English.

"You're gonna read?" Marty demanded.

"You need my help?" Harry asked.

"Of course not!"

"Then I'm gonna read."

"Bastard," Marty said as he stood up.

The three Hispanics were enjoying their moment of macho pride. They had an entire American jetliner at their disposal. All the fat and rich capitalists were frightened.

Juan Esposito watched as the skinny, funny-looking American pushed aside the curtain and entered the tourist section from the first-class cabin.

"You, back in your seat," Esposito said loudly, and in a commanding tone that the nuns used to use when he went to school. It was the first time he'd gotten to order a passenger about, and it felt good, so he did it again. "Back in your seat."

"I gotta take a shit." The little blond man seemed to be challenging Juan. That wouldn't do. Juan moved toward him and pushed a straight arm against the flat chest of the American.

Marty fell backward, and that gave him just enough time to see what was what. To gauge how much strength the terrorist was willing to use against a passenger, and how much more strength there might be in his arm. To see that one of Juan's friends had a small electronic device in his hand. That explained it. They hadn't tried to bring arms on board the plane. There was just a bomb in the baggage compartment that could be triggered from the electronic signal from that black box. It was being held—carefully—by the man directly behind Juan in the aisle. Marty remembered some stuff Cowboy had told him, and then he made some quick calculations about the men's positions.

"American faggot, back to your seat!"

All the careful plans that Marty had been making were erased in that instant. "Did you really call me a faggot?"

"Yeah, you piece of garbage, get back to your seat now or I—"

Juan never finished the sentence. Marty's palm had gone

straight into his nose. The little guy had more power than anyone on that plane—except for Harry—would have given him credit for. Marty's muscles were bound in a slender, rickety-looking body, but they were strong and tight. They had all the power in them of months and months of training under a mean son-of-a-bitch Cherokee ex-marine.

Juan's nose shattered, splintered, and made a trip of a couple of inches to a place where it had never been before. In the middle of Juan's brain. Where it had a short vacation, and looked around, and then caused Juan Esposito to die.

Juan's body collapsed onto the carpeted floor. Bits of his brain, mixed with blood, boiled up out of Juan's slack mouth.

The sight momentarily stunned the other two Hispanics. They weren't prepared for this. They hadn't brought guns because they wouldn't need them, and they hadn't figured out a way to get them past the metal detectors. They had knives that were made of hard plastic, but Americans were so frightened of violence that—

Their hesitation, and their thoughts on Americans' dislike of violence, was a great mistake. It gave Marty enough time to get a couple of big jumps into his run, enough time to have his legs in the air in front of his body and to deliver his feet into the chest of the second man. The black box dropped to the ground and rolled backward. A child in the middle section of seats reached down and picked it up, but his mother took it away from him and put it on the empty seat on the other side of her.

Marty had knocked down the second man in the aisle. Twice he jumped on the man's chest, bringing down the heel of his new cowboy boot sharply against the man's ribs. Marty had developed an instinct for this sort of thing—even the Black Berets didn't get all that much practice in breaking a man's ribs. But Marty still succeeded, and one of the broken ribs sliced open the left lung and two chambers of the man's heart and he died. Marty jumped one last time and the man was finished.

The third Hispanic was cowering in the back corner of the cabin, pushing against the door of one of the restrooms. He waved his plastic knife vaguely in front of him.

"Bastard!" Marty screamed as he moved toward him. The man threw aside the knife and tumbled forward on his knees.

"Please, please," he prayed, as he once had prayed to the Virgin to forgive him for masturbating three times a day. He'd gone to the same school as Juan Esposito.

Marty grabbed the man by his hair and dragged him down the aisle to where the two corpses lay. Already the passengers had evacuated that portion of the plane—Marty's work was unappetizing. He whipped off the belts of the two men and used them to bind the survivor.

Then he dragged the man back down the aisle, and pushed him into one of the restroom cubicles, and kicked shut the door. Then he located the black box on the empty seat and quickly dismantled it.

"All right," he said when he finished, "somebody tell the pilot to turn—"

But there was applause for him, drowning out his words.

Thunderous applause that turned his pale skin a bright red.

Not knowing how to handle it, he went back to the corpses, lifted them up, and pushed them into a couple of window seats. The stewardess he had lusted after came as close as she dared and handed him a couple of blankets, which he threw over the two bodies.

The applause went on. The stewardess, now spared the sight of the corpses, threw her arms around Marty, pressed her ample breasts against his chest, and kissed him long and hard on the mouth.

His blush became a deeper, fiercer red when she finally let go, and he staggered toward the first-class section again.

"I need a drink," he murmured—and that brought on another round of applause.

He pushed aside the curtains and dropped into the seat next to Harry.

"Well, I did it—" he began. But Harry was asleep, with his head on his shoulder and the boring pro-Communist pamphlet open on his knee.

# 3

"Why do you need those computers just to balance a goddamn checkbook? Damn it! Shouldn't even be using a check-book. Cash on hand and a pile of deeds on top of them—that's the way it should be."

Cowboy looked up from the sheaf of printouts that the computers had generated for him an hour ago. He'd been sitting in the living room studying them ever since, sipping at a beer now and then, but, more often than not, forgetting that he had the drink.

"You are amazing," Cowboy finally said. "If you had your way, we'd be back in the stone age, trading pieces of shell for what you couldn't get fishing or hunting. Beeker, if we had 'cash on hand,' there wouldn't be room enough in this house to put up our bunks. You got any idea how much money we got?"

"Too much," Beeker growled. "Makes us soft. Next thing you know you and Rosie are gonna want to hire stand-ins for your training."

Cowboy grinned. "We already tried. Nobody'd take the job—no matter how much money we offered. Nobody but a fool forged in hell is gonna train under you, Billy Leaps."

"Right," said Beeker. "So what's all that crap?" He contemptuously indicated the printouts in Cowboy's lap.

"Our investments," said Cowboy. It was amazing—here they were, five guys who eighteen months before couldn't have raised ten thousand dollars if every one of them had gone out on the corner to beg. And here they were now—an international corporation, headquartered in the Seychelles, with investments in a dozen foreign countries. Each of them had a numbered bank account in Switzerland. Each of them had a safety-deposit box in Shreveport that was stuffed with diamonds.

They didn't need it, of course. They could have gotten by on a tenth of what they earned in a year—and gotten by more handsomely than any of them ever imagined would have been possible. Harry could have bought twenty bars like the one he had walked out of. Rosie could have endowed a new hospital for Newark twice as big as the one he used to work at. Cowboy could have any kind of plane he wanted, except the ones that were still covered by the government secrecy acts. Applebaum could have bought buildings to blow up, though he'd still just have to pretend that there were sharpshooters crouching beneath every windowsill.

It was Beeker who complained so much about the money they made—almost despite themselves—but it was Beeker who spent more than all the rest of them put together. Because Beeker bought land every chance he got.

"All this is illegal," said Beeker quietly. "You do all that shit with Delilah, and we don't even have to pay taxes on it. Man ought to pay his taxes."

"Oh, right," said Cowboy. "Every Cherokee who's ever been thrown off a reservation ought to pay for the lawyers who got a judge to sign the decree to take away all their land. Oh yeah, the government's treated you real good, Beak. Treated your boy good too. Remember?"

Billy Leaps remembered all right. Remembered how Tsali had been shuffled from orphanage to foster home to juvenile detention center and then to another foster home that was twice as bad as the first one had been. Remembered that Tsali had never received adequate instruction to overcome his handicap. Had never gotten anything in his life except the wrong end of the stick. Beeker remembered that, all right.

"The problem is," Cowboy went on, "that we just can't waltz down to the IRS and claim our income. 'Hello, Mr. Agent, I got this money by offing two hundred Indonesian terrorists in New Neuzen. Great beaches in New Neuzen, Mr. Agent, especially now that they've mopped up the blood. And this four hundred thousand? Oh, right, that's that revolution in South America. Well, part of that came from the CIA, and they told me it wasn't supposed to be taxable. Maybe you ought to call up the head, tell him, "Billy Leaps sent me." I've done work for him before. Oh, right, and now we're gonna declare about a million dollars' depreciation on a couple of thousand karats of uncut diamonds. Oh, diamonds don't depreciate? Well, that's—'" Cowboy broke off. "See what I mean? We'd have a little problem, even if we were straight with the government. Let me tell you something, Beeker, they don't *want* us coming in. Because if they did, we'd hear about it. And we ain't never had any trouble from the IRS. If you don't trust me, trust Delilah. She set all this up. Get off my back."

Tsali entered the room at that moment, drawn there by the angry voices of Cowboy and his father. He glanced at his father, and then went over to Cowboy's chair and peered over his shoulder at the printouts, as if curious.

"You want me to explain some of this to you?" Cowboy asked.

Tsali nodded.

Beeker turned away, the angry words he had prepared to throw against Cowboy fading on his lips.

Tsali had a power they all recognized and all respected. Whenever the verbal battles between team members got nearly out of hand, he would walk in and—simply by his presence, or some simple action—pour oil upon the troubled waters.

His curiosity about the printouts had altered the situation.

Beeker was growling, but he moved away and sat at the baronial table, on which they ate their meals and spread their maps and made their plans for the next assignment.

Billy Leaps—still no smile on his face—spread out a large chart. It was from the office of the local assessor and showed the ownership of all the real estate in the county. In colored inks he had marked off different sections of the map.

The original holding of his farm.

The secondary and contiguous acquisitions.

The newest acquisition, which didn't border the principal property.

And finally, outlined in purple, the two different plots that would serve to connect the properties.

One belonged to an oil company and the other to a manufacturer of cardboard cartons, headquartered in Massachusetts. Neither company would even consider selling Beeker the land he coveted.

It was these purple parcels that captured Beeker's attention now, just as they had for the past two months.

Tsali seemed to sense just when he should change from one station in the house to another. Cowboy was calmed down, the attacks on the investments he took such pleasure in overseeing had been diverted. But Billy Leaps was still in need. The kid came over and stood beside his adoptive father.

There were some similarities between the two of them. Tsali

was a full-blooded Cherokee, one who hadn't had his bloodlines diluted with Anglo interbreeding. Beeker had. His blue eyes betrayed his mother's nationality. But the hair on Beeker's head was just as black and his cheekbones just as high and prominent as Tsali's. The kid's skin was darker, but Billy Leaps had the olive complexion sure enough.

Tsali was still growing. He wasn't yet as tall as his father, but there was some probability he'd make it to those six feet. If he kept eating and exercising with the same intensity as he had this past year and a half he'd certainly get the bulk, with the same definition as his father's.

The proximity of his son seemed to relax Beeker. Tsali dropped down on his haunches, and Beeker put an arm around the boy's shoulder. Then, with his free hand, he ran along the outline of the new property, outlined in orange.

It represented a hundred seventeen acres—his largest single purchase. The land around Shreveport had been divided up among small landowners for a couple of hundred years. Beeker had become one of the largest landholders of the area, but it was nearly impossible to buy any substantial amount at any one time. This parcel had belonged to a logging company that had fallen on hard times—it was forced to sell off a portion of its resources, the forested land. Beeker had paid dearly for it and had had to concede one final spurt of logging on the property. But once the trees were cleared and the land planted again, it would be his.

Cowboy had pointed out, of course, that this property had nothing at all to recommend it. It was expensive. It would be bare by the time it came into Beeker's hands, and wouldn't be real forest for another fifteen or twenty years. It had two tiny ponds and no real running water, only one access road, and through some strange provenance, higher taxes than any of the surrounding properties.

Didn't matter.

The land was up for sale, it was near Beeker's holdings, so Beeker wanted it.

And Beeker, having the money, bought it.

"Who's gonna call?" said Beeker.

"Call who?" said Cowboy.

"Call these people who own this other property," said Beeker. "Maybe you should, Cowboy. You're better at shit like that. You call 'em up, find out how much they want for it. Don't like the idea of being surrounded by all these other people."

"Nearest house is four miles away," Cowboy pointed out.

"Yeah," said Beeker thoughtfully, "but how can Tsali and me set up a marathon course unless we get these two corridor properties?"

"You want to set up your own marathon course?" Cowboy asked, incredulous.

"Right," said Beeker.

Tsali grinned and nodded vigorously. It may not have been his idea, but he was eager to go along with it.

"You don't have the money," said Cowboy, winking at Tsali.

"What the hell do you mean?" said Beeker, turning savagely to his friend. "You just said—"

"I gotta do some figuring," said Cowboy. "Talk to Delilah. Yeah, well, maybe if she and I do some work with this corporation—this corporation owned and operated by the Black Berets Incorporated—then maybe we'll be able to squeeze out enough money for you to buy up that land. Build you a marathon course."

"Well, goddamn it, Cowboy, if you like looking at those goddamn figures every day the way you do—"

"I get a kick out of it," said Cowboy. "Not like I get a kick out of cocaine, but it'll do. I can't keep cocaine around here, anyway—"

"You sure as hell can't!"

"—'cause Tsali always steals it. Snorts it up before—"

Tsali looked panicked for a second—to be accused of something he'd never even *think* of doing. He looked to his father with a tortured expression, as if to say, *No, I'd never—*

But the expression on Billy Leaps's face showed that he clearly saw through Cowboy's little joke.

Then Tsali laughed too.

"All right," said Cowboy. "You let me work with these figures awhile, Beeker, and I'll get you enough money to buy this whole damn county. And you and Tsali can run twenty-six goddamn miles a day and never see another human being—if that is gonna be your idea of a good time."

"It is," said Beeker. "And, in fact, that is just what we are gonna do right now."

He rolled up the map, and then he and Tsali disappeared for a few minutes. When they returned they were dressed only in running shorts and shoes.

"Where's Rosie?" Billy Leaps asked.

"In Shreveport, picking up some barbequed chicken, I believe. Rosie got a sudden crave on for barbeque. And a crave for the lady that turns the spit. He said he'd be back in a couple of hours."

Beeker nodded, and then he and his son went out the door. Their run began right on the doorstep.

Cowboy got up and stood at the screen door and watched them as they leaped the pasture fence and took off across the newly mown field.

He shook his head at them, wonderingly, then went to the refrigerator and got out another bottle of beer. He hadn't finished the first one, but it was warm. Then he spread the printouts across the table and laughed out loud, just thinking about how goddamn rich he had become.

# 4

Harry watched Marty as he strode across the floor of the huge, glittering, crowded casino. He'd seen a walk like that before. On a Louisiana farm near Beeker's—it was the way the cock marched out of the henhouse after another conquest. Marty looked just as natural and just as ridiculous.

Harry supposed Marty had a right to it. After all, he had one of the most beautiful women in the place on his arm. She wasn't quite as tall as Applebaum, but her red hair was piled so high that she appeared to be so. It didn't matter to either of them. They were oblivious to the stares and comments as they moved through the crowds.

Marty had finally gotten a woman. After he'd halted the hijacking, that stewardess had thought he was the most wonderful man in the world. It hadn't hurt that he'd been flying first class in the company of a man listed on the passenger roll as Harry the Greek. As soon as she'd discovered that the little man was going to be in Las Vegas for a week, she'd arranged a little paid leave—to recover from the trauma of the incident.

She looked pretty much recovered.

Harry should have been happy. For several reasons. Marty was his friend and Marty was happy. Maureen on Marty's arm meant that Harry wasn't being called on every ten seconds to look at something, or respond to something, or listen to some story he'd heard a thousand times before. For one vacation at least Harry would be able to sit and sip Scotch in silence and solitude—or as much solitude and silence as one ever found in a casino that could hold five thousand people and was open twenty-four hours a day and had a decibel level that was about equivalent to that of the interior of a jet engine. But silence and solitude were relative. He could pull the handle on a few slots, drink some more. Play a couple of hands of blackjack, drink some more. Sit by the pool and drink some more. Perfect vacation. But Harry'd never been good at allowing pleasure to flood in on him, and he really didn't quite know how to be happy.

So Harry was deep in depression. About Marty's good fortune. He wasn't jealous, of course. Not of Marty's temporary fame aboard the plane, not of his conquest of the very delectable Maureen. Harry wasn't even upset that it was he—and not Marty—who'd had to deal with the authorities and explain why it would not be a good idea at all for Marty's name to get into the paper. No, Harry was depressed thinking about what was going to happen after the week with Maureen was over. After all the years of listening to Applebaum's stories about women—stories that had been sheerest fabrication and wish—now the bastard was going to have something real to brag about. If he could construct hours of detail over sexual conquests that had never happened except in his fevered brain, what would he be capable of now, with honest raw material? With a stewardess yet? Mind-boggling. So mind-boggling that Harry decided he'd better have another drink.

He walked over to the other side of the casino and entered one of the numerous small bars that fringed the playing room.

This was serious business and called for a serious volume of Scotch. He wanted to be leaning on the bar rail himself, not dependent on the services of the army of cocktail waitresses with soft costumes, and firm bodies, and hard faces.

With a good tall glass of Black Label on ice in his hand, Harry was almost content. He shrugged off a couple of women who approached him, not even bothering to check their intent. He didn't care if they were b-girls hustling drinks for the management, hookers looking for action in one of the hundreds and hundreds of rooms piled up above this casino, or just honest women after a bit of quiet, impassioned companionship. Harry liked women, no question about that. And women liked Harry. They were drawn to his size, his muscular, hairy body, and his deep, sad eyes. He was a man who looked as if he didn't need a woman—which to a woman was a sure sign that he needed a woman very very badly—so it wasn't anything special to have them flurry his way, like gaily-colored moths swarming around a candle flame. When he wanted a woman, there'd be one there. Harry never understood men who felt a need to take every woman who came their way. Wasteful.

It wasn't wasteful to get another glass of Scotch. The bartender saw the way Harry pushed the glass across the wooden surface and automatically came back with the Johnny Walker bottle, not even looking into Harry's eyes for confirmation. Certainly not speaking. He free-poured a triple over the ice and rang up the charge on the check in silence. Even put the check out of sight beside the register. Harry liked that. Good bartenders treated different customers differently. When Harry had owned a bar, that's the kind of bartender he had been. With any luck, this one wouldn't exchange a single word with Harry until it was time to pay off the tab. If then.

Crowds in Las Vegas were weird, Harry thought. Most

conspicuous were the men who dragged around overly made-up women, all trying to convince the crowd in general that they were important and rich. The men who looked over their shoulders to see who was looking at them. If you were really important, of course, you wouldn't care *what* a lot of nonentities thought about you anyway—right? The car dealers from Pomona, the insurance brokers from Peoria, the bar owners from Knoxville—all of them had come to this place to compete with one another.

The real rich weren't even noticing the ones who played at it. Harry could tell them by the emotionless faces of the women, afraid to smile or blink lest their facelifts drop to the floor and smash like glass. The rich men were quietly mannered, as if afraid of being noticed—as if God were roaming the clouds with a thunderbolt looking out for mortals who'd been given greater than their share of earthly wealth. Quiet dress, quiet manners—but not many of that kind of people in Vegas. Probably too tacky for them, Harry decided. They'd be up in the lakeside places at Tahoe.

Then there were the serious gamblers. More often than not they were the ones who came into the barroom desperate for a drink. You could tell by their faces and their lurching gait that they'd lost. Lost not only the money—that was just what got thrown down on the table in the form of brightly colored rounds of plastic—but lost other things too. Their kids' college educations. Their cars. Their houses. Their marriages. That's why they staggered toward the liquor. It helped, and it was about the only thing they could afford anymore. Harry understood them the best. He'd lost a lot in his life, and the money he was accumulating as a Black Beret was never going to make up for it.

Then there were the lucky ones who just came to Vegas to have a good time. Rosie would have fit in with them. They had a certain amount of money they could play with. Some won, most of them lost, but never too much in either direction. They had women, but the women were companions, not display mannequins. They walked through the crowds obviously not caring whether they were noticed or not. Harry was a little jealous of them. It would be nice to go through life like that. Not paying much attention to what was going on. Not much affected by what had occurred in the past. Not caring an awful lot what was going to happen tomorrow.

The barkeep was doing just fine. Harry was going to have to leave a big tip. Anyone who'd pour two triple Black Labels without a single word was a treasure. He made a mental note. Marty was sure to drag him back to Vegas again. Applebaum loved the glitz of the place, and now he'd be hoping for another hijack, another Maureen as reward. When they did come back next time, they'd have to stay in this very same hotel so Harry could drink in this particular bar and get served by this one bartender.

That's how you could tell a real alcoholic—he was always laying plans for the next drink.

Depressing thought.

Harry swallowed more Scotch.

A crowd of men entered the room just then. Harry looked up to check them out, wondering which category of gambler they were. Gamblers didn't mix. The types stuck together.

The four guys were the easy ones, the ones who just had a good time and didn't have to worry if they dropped a couple thou. Their houses weren't going to get repossessed and their kids weren't going to go without an education. Just guys with a few bucks to throw around. Then Harry seemed to wake up.

He knew one of the men.

Jack Seeley.

He'd been one of the hired hands on that farm in South Texas—hell, Harry couldn't even remember the name of it now—the place where the Black Berets had last fought, the place where they'd coptered in and destroyed an army of right-wing fanatics led by an oil-rich Texan. Fat Texan. Couldn't remember his name either. Anyway, this was Seeley, who'd flown the copter.

They'd hated that, the Black Berets. It was Cowboy who should be flying them in. But Cowboy had been held prisoner, and they were trying to rescue him. Seeley was one of the Black Berets' prisoners, and he had to fill in.

He'd come through. Harry had always wondered about that, that and what happened afterward. Seeley and Beeker had a talk, that's all Harry knew. Whatever had been said, it had ended the good feelings between this flyboy and the Berets. Harry never found out what had been said, what had gone on between the two men. He only knew that afterward, Beeker had been more silent than usual. And that was saying something.

Seeley was ordering a drink now. He caught a glimpse of Harry, and something in the way his shoulders hunched told Harry the man was on edge. He was ignoring his pals' laughing conversation. As soon as his drink was delivered, he walked over to Harry. "Beeker here?"

Harry shook his head no.

Seeley looked at him. "You expect him sometime soon?"

Again, no.

"Tell him I meant it, stay out of my way."

"Where's he going to bump into you?"

"I just know he's going to. He'll be sorry. Real sorry." Seeley turned and walked out of the bar. He hadn't even taken a sip of his drink, or spoken a word of good-bye to his friends.

Those men watched Seeley leave in astonishment, and then they turned their gaze on Harry. Harry didn't even look at them. He raised a single finger, and that very good silent bartender poured another triple.

# 5

Beeker and Tsali ran back to the house. They were both deeply winded, both drenched with sweat. In some places on their bodies the perspiration had captured the Louisiana dust, leaving a veneer of mud caked there.

They began their cool-down. A repeat of some of the exercises that had started their hearts pumping for the long run was necessary to calm that same heartbeat down to manageable numbers. They were well into them, their breathing already more relaxed, when Beeker suddenly stopped. He'd just seen something different about the place.

Tsali sensed his father's startled motionlessness and looked around. What was different was a car. Off to the side of the house was a circular swath of concrete with half a dozen vehicles on it. Beeker's pickup, dented and dirty. The red Corvette that Cowboy had just bought—he'd told Beeker it was for himself, but Tsali knew it was there just waiting for the license he'd get the next month. Rosie's sky-blue Cadillac. Marty's little open-topped MG—the better to see you with, my dear. The usual. And off to the side, nearly hidden, a big

Cougar. The kind of car that's bought up by rental agencies and nobody else.

"Good morning."

Typical of her to walk out of the house at the very moment they'd discovered her presence.

Delilah.

The woman in their lives. Tsali thought she had to be the most beautiful woman in the world. Not a whole lot of men who'd argue with him about that. White skin that never burned or even turned pink, deep-red lipstick that painted her mouth like a target. Blond hair, thick and just slightly waved. Her dresses were not only stylish, they were works of engineering perfection. How else could they be made of such soft material, encircle her tiny waist so delicately, and yet hold up those large, round mounds on her chest?

And there was her scent.

Tsali could smell it now. Always the same. A scent that told of flowers and open spaces, purity and sensuality all at once. It was Delilah's signature. Literally. She didn't bother signing her letters. The fragrance when the envelope was opened told who it was from. He remembered it on those occasional notes that arrived at the farm, in rooms that she had just left, even on his father's body—very slightly—after they'd . . .

He blushed deeply that he would even think that about his father and Delilah.

He poked Beeker and signed: *I'm going in to clean up.*

Billy Leaps nodded, ruffling Tsali's hair with quiet affection.

"No you don't." Delilah stopped the boy as he tried to creep past her. She had him by the shoulder, and despite the slippery sheen of sweat there, her grip held. She brushed her cheek against his. He felt as if he'd been dipped head-first into the bottle that held her perfume. When she drew away, he had tasted a new taste—that of the lipstick she wore. He wouldn't soon forget that either. The other thing he felt, of course, was the blood that had risen to his face, burning him with embarrassment. Delilah didn't laugh at that, didn't even appear to notice it. Tsali hurried inside, leaving the woman and his father alone together.

When Tsali had closed the front door behind himself, Delilah walked down the few stairs and stood in front of Billy Leaps. She was wearing heels. They sank slightly into the soft clay. The Cherokee hadn't spoken or moved to greet her. Just stood there. But as though to protect himself against her approach, he had crossed his arms over his chest. It made him suddenly appear to be one of his ancestors, standing with only a swatch of cloth around his midsection. Gleaming with sweat, half his ear torn off in some distant battle, his arms held in that position, he could have been a model for the Indian on a new version of the buffalo nickel.

The crossed arms didn't stop Delilah. She came right up to him. The fabric of her dress grazed his forearms, and he had to brace himself not to shiver as if touched with cold. She was only five three and had to crane her neck to look him in the eye.

When he looked down to her, he could see not only the creamy white skin of her face and the blood-red mouth, but he had a pretty good view down the front of her blouse as well.

What this time? Beeker wondered. The woman was always pulling something new. Something new on him and something new on the Black Berets as well. He often mistrusted her, or tried to. No other female had ever breached the defenses of Billy Leaps Beeker the way Delilah had. Every time he saw her, there was a new angle of attack, a new strategy that turned him into a shaven Samson. What would she want this time?

Delilah's eyes left his and her head moved closer toward him. Her small tongue, so pink, darted out and licked a morsel of sweat off his chest. Delicately, like a child licking a raindrop from a windowpane. Once, twice. Then it moved quickly over to one of his nipples and sucked in the hard flesh. Delilah had a trick—a deliberate one, Beeker was certain—of doing things that would have made any other woman attempting them appear a slut. But not her. The movement of her tongue wasn't cheap, it was as if she were saying, I'm a connoisseur of perspiration. I'm trying Cherokee this morning. She might have been tasting wine, filling her glass from the spigot in the oaken cask.

A man should know when he's defeated, when he should retreat to regroup his forces in order to do battle again someday. This was a battle that Beeker couldn't win. The pressure against the elastic in his jockstrap was his banner of defeat. Once more Delilah had defeated him on their personal battleground.

He moved back and in one motion gathered her up in his arms. She smiled that special smile that was her quiet trumpet of victory. Always one smile, lasting no more than a second or two. A smile not repeated. A smile that made Billy Leaps Beeker feel as if he'd just had his soul ground down into the Louisiana dirt.

He walked up the stairs and kicked open the door. Rosie was in the kitchen, rummaging in the refrigerator. Tsali wasn't around. He carried her down the corridor onto which all the bunkrooms opened in a long line of narrow doors. One for each of the six males who lived in the house. Each one just the same—a military cot, a chest of drawers, a chair and desk. That's all a man needed, that's all a man who lived there got. Beeker's was in the middle of the line.

He carried her in and laid her carefully on the single bed. She lifted up her midsection, reached down, and pulled off the narrow silk garment that clung wetly there.

"Don't you want me to shower?" he asked, conscious of his smell in the tiny room. He suddenly thought of his two wives and what *they* thought of the Cherokee brand of perspiration.

"You're just the way I want you," said Delilah. "The way I want you *now*."

# 6

Tsali never knew how to act at times like this. He went over to the kitchen sink and ran the faucet, picking up the cleanser and making it appear as though he were about to start scrubbing the stainless steel basin.

They were walking down the corridor. He had known they'd be coming because the shower had stopped just a few minutes ago. They'd have toweled off now, unless they'd started again . . .

The blush burned his face. He knew about what they were doing. Cowboy had initiated him into that secret in a whorehouse on New Neuzen. But the fact is, he'd killed more often than he'd fucked, and the whole thing was still a mystery to him. Especially when he thought about his father doing it with Delilah.

Even if Billy Leaps had wanted to be discreet about the matter, he wouldn't have been able to. The house wasn't large, the interior walls weren't thick. This wasn't a house for secrets. It was a house for men to do what they did out in the open.

Sex was a good thing, a fine thing, a thing that a man and a woman should do when they liked each other—or even when they just wanted sex. Why did Tsali get so embarrassed just because his father and Delilah were doing it in the same house he was in? Why couldn't he just read a book and not pay attention to the noise?

Delilah was the first. He smelled her perfume before he heard her voice. Billy Leaps was right behind her. Whenever they were finished doing . . . *it*, Tsali's father always seemed content, more relaxed than he was at any other time. Or it had always seemed that way before. Maybe this time was the exception.

As the two of them took seats on a couch facing the big fireplace in the living area, Tsali could actually see Beeker's neck muscles knotting in tension.

Delilah wasn't even settled before Beeker challenged her. "What do you want this time?"

Delilah kept her smile. She crossed her arms and self-indulgently rubbed her shoulders beneath the short robe she was wearing. "Don't I get offered a drink? A glass of wine?" she asked over her shoulder at Tsali.

"Tsali," said his father. A command.

"And one for your father," said Delilah.

"No," said Beeker.

Tsali went to the refrigerator and took out the bottle of white wine that Cowboy kept there. The flier had taught him how to remove the cork, and he did this carefully. He found the right kind of glass and brought the drink to Delilah.

"Thanks," she said.

"Find something to do," said his father shortly. Meaning, get out.

Tsali got out.

Delilah sipped at her wine. "The boy could have stayed. I thought you were teaching him to grow up without secrets."

"I want to know what you want." She'd beaten him on the first round. He intended to win this one.

"Maybe I came down to visit. My five strange friends and my little boy."

"He's not a little boy anymore," said Beeker.

Delilah smiled. "Remember you said that. Maybe I just came down here to get laid."

"You could get that in D.C."

"I'm rich," she said. "I don't mind traveling for quality."

"Come clean," he said.

"We need you. We need all of you."

*We* again. She'd never said who *we* were. *We* was Delilah, and behind Delilah one man, or five hundred men, or one agency, or the entire armed forces. Beeker might never find out. But Delilah always said *we*.

Beeker said nothing. He waited. She didn't hurry. She sipped her wine. She stretched her neck and smiled contentedly. As if she were a career woman on a ski weekend who'd managed to bed the handsome instructor.

"San Sebastian," she said. "You know it?"

"Never been there." But he knew about it—a small country in Central America, borders with two or three others, short coastline on the Gulf of Mexico, mestizo population, and—against all probability—a democratic government.

"But you know it," she said, as if she'd read his thoughts. "And you know that it's been stable for nearly a quarter of a century now. It's practically the only country down there we haven't made a fool of ourselves over—the only one we've never really had to worry about."

She paused, and Beeker said, "But you're worried now."

"Otherwise I wouldn't be here, talking about it."

"What's the danger?"

She shook her head. "We're not sure. But the danger's real. We're convinced of that. And we're also convinced that the present government—a real government, of the people, by the people, and so on—has to stay in power. But the American military's overextended in El Salvador and Honduras as it is. If there was even a *hint* that we were involved in the internal affairs of yet another Central American country, the U.S. Senate would have a collective heart attack."

Beeker nodded, with a slight wry smile, as if the thought pleased him. It did.

"And no matter how attractive an image that might be to you, I'd like for you to prevent it."

He shook his head. "We're tired. We've had enough for a while. Hire some mercs."

"I intend to. The Black Berets."

His eyes widened and filled with anger. "We aren't mercs, we're—"

"You go on missions and you collect money. You've collected a great deal of money. I ought to know, I've helped Cowboy invest it."

"We didn't collect that money in fees," said Beeker.

That was true. They'd never been directly paid for any of the work they'd accomplished. But in every case, there'd been some dirty little stash of cash or securities or diamonds that had belonged to nobody but the men who were now dead—and that's how the Black Berets got rich. Not on fees from some unnamed and unnamable government source.

"I know that. And I'm not offering you a fee for this. I'm offering—"

"There's nothing you can offer that would make me take on this—"

Delilah rode over his objection as if he'd not spoken at all. "I'm offering two hundred acres of land. That's all."

Billy Leaps paused. "What two hundred acres?"

"A little parcel of land near here. Very near here. I've come to a little arrangement with a Mr. Dooley—"

The man from the cardboard container corporation who Beeker couldn't even get in to speak to. The man who controlled the sales of the timberland that was contiguous to his own. The land that would link the two major parcels of his farm holdings.

Delilah had won again.

"How much?" he said. "How much do I have to pay for it? Dooley wouldn't even discuss it with me. So how much is that land?—and I'll pay it."

"No money," said Delilah. "All I need is a simple yes. You'll go on the mission. At the end of the mission, I turn over the deeds."

Beeker thought for a moment, thinking about his marathon track and about pushing the world even farther away than it was now. Then, glancing away, not looking at Delilah directly, he asked, "What's the deal?"

That should have been enough to bring back that smile of triumph he'd seen entirely too often. But it didn't. Instead of smiling, Delilah frowned. She looked away. She got up and refilled her wine glass.

There was more to this . . .

"The president of San Sebastian is in danger. He's about to make a visit to Washington, and everything we have says there's going to be an assassination attempt. We don't know what direction it's to come from though. We want maximum security, and so far as I'm concerned, that means you. I want you to come back to D.C. with me and act as his bodyguard."

"And . . ."

There was bound to be more.

"And we have to set up a force of Black Berets in San Sebastian. They have to have perfect cover, and be ready for just about anything."

"Harry and Marty are in Vegas. They'll be back in a couple of days."

"Can't wait that long," said Delilah. "I want somebody down there *now*."

"But we can't leave the farm unguarded." It was a cardinal rule that one of them should be on the Louisiana property at all times. "There's only Cowboy and Rosie. That'd mean only one of them could go to San Sebastian—"

"No," said Delilah. "Two of them could go. Rosie and Tsali."

# 7

Beeker's face went blank, as if he were in a state of shock. He hadn't even considered the possibility. Of course he knew the time would come eventually, but not now. Not yet. The kid had just turned seventeen. "You're not—"

"Serious? It's perfect. There's a Third World track meet going on down there. Starts in two days. Tsali's a great runner. He ought to be—you trained him. He's a full-blooded Indian. Third World as they come. And with Rosie as his coach, nobody'd give those two a second thought."

"Tsali's never competed," Beeker protested. It was all he could think to say.

Delilah laughed. "That's just like you. I'm not trying to enter him to *win*, I'm just trying to enter him to pass as a contestant. It's not going to matter if he comes in last or next to last."

Beeker wanted to say, Tsali would never come in last, no matter what race he entered, but that would be playing into Delilah's hands. He said nothing.

"I've arranged for the name of Tsali Leaps Beeker to be placed on the American team."

"Already?" Beeker's voice was quiet. The word had many meanings just now.

Delilah nodded. *Already*. She'd gone ahead, gambling that Beeker would consent. *Already*. It was time for Tsali to join the team.

"No," he said.

"Tsali is the perfect in for the Berets," said Delilah. "There's no reason for Americans to go to San Sebastian at this time of year other than the track meet. He and Rosie will—"

"No."

"Let's ask him."

"He's only seventeen! There's no—"

"When you were seventeen you'd finished three months of marine training and you were on your way to Vietnam." She said it quietly. But the truth stabbed.

"There isn't anything going on in San Sebastian that would be worth my son's life," said Beeker.

"It's time for him to start his life."

Like a mother and father arguing over their boy's education.

Beeker wanted to say, That's not going to be his life. But that was bullshit and he knew it. It *was* Tsali's life. A year ago they'd left him alone on the farm while they'd all gone to Africa. He was guarding the house. They had thought it was just a way to make him feel important. To show they trusted him. But when three men had attacked the place, Tsali didn't know his role was a sham. He'd killed two of them with a bow and arrow. Slit the third one's throat.

There was no way to erase that experience. When a kid's killed for his father, taken a human life to protect his homestead, he's been committed to a warrior's life. Already. And forever.

He had been blooded.

Since he'd come to live with Beeker he'd trained constantly.

Not just in the sports that would increase his coordination and endurance, but in killing. He could handle an M-16 with the proficiency of a marine marksman now. He could throw a knife like one of the ancient Cherokee tribesmen.

Who am I fooling? Beeker asked himself. He looked out the window at his land. So many acres of it already! He suddenly realized that the reason he kept buying it was in a vain hope that with enough ditches, and fences, and electronic sentries, and money in the bank, he and Tsali and the others could keep out the rest of the world.

Stupid hope.

"Ask Tsali," he said to Delilah. "It's his decision."

An hour later there was a knock on the door of Billy Leaps's room. He didn't answer. He listened. The knock was repeated.

"Come," he said.

Tsali pushed open the door and came in. Beeker was lying down on the cot. Tsali seated himself cross-legged on the floor. A stance of rest, meditation, decision.

*Tell me what to do*, he signed.

"No. I've made enough decisions. I decided you should have the skills. I decided that you could live with a bunch of crazy assholes who think their M-16s are alive. I decided that you should learn nothing but what five killers could teach you. I decided—"

*You made me a warrior.*

Beeker shook his head. "I've given you the chance. That's all."

*I want your—*

He spelled a word Billy Leaps didn't recognize at first. Then he cast back his memory and remembered that his grandmother had used it once.

Blessing.

Tsali wanted his blessing.

"You have my blessing, whatever you decide."

Tsali sat for a moment, his eyes cast down. Then he looked up at his father again.

*If I go south, will you go with Delilah?*

"Yeah, I guess I will," Beeker admitted. Why would he go to D.C.? Because of Delilah? Or because it was action? Action, the drug that the five of them had all become addicted to, the drug they had introduced into Tsali's veins themselves. It was a drug exhilarating as heroin, but it was one that you could never go cold turkey on. You couldn't ease out of it either—kill one fewer bad guys every day for a month, and then you were free. It was injected and it stayed.

*Then I will go with Rosie. I will be safe.*

"I'll kill Rosie if anything happens to you."

*If anything happened to me, Rosie would already be dead.*

Beeker looked at Tsali and understood. He was a member of the team now, and the time had come for him to join one of the team's missions. It couldn't be put off any longer.

"One thing," said Beeker.

Tsali looked up. Absolute trust. Absolute obedience.

"Whatever you do, whatever happens down there—you're not doing it for Delilah, you understand? You're doing it for me. For your father."

# 8

Rosie and Tsali sat in the big first-class seats of the airliner that was carrying them from New Orleans to Huasteca, the capital of San Sebastian. Rosie had a tall glass of bourbon in his hand. Damn good thing they flew first class so he didn't have to screw around with any of those little tiny plastic cups the others in the back of the plane would be getting. He had a man-size drink in an honest-to-God glass.

He took a sip of the liquor, good shit, the best. Used to be that Rosie'd drink any kind of liquor that called itself bourbon if it was cheap enough. Those were the days when he hardly had two pennies to rub together in his pocket. Now he was rich, richer than an undertaker with a Harlem street-corner monopoly. That was *terrible* rich, as his mama used to say.

He sighed and looked out the little window of the 727. Too bad this wasn't one of the real big ones, a 747. That'd be better. But this little country, San Sebastian; it probably didn't have enough people to fill up one of those monsters for the return trip. Probably didn't have an airstrip long enough for a 747 to set down on. The 727 was okay, anyway, as long as you were going first class.

It'd be nice to think they were going on a little beach vacation. Just him and the kid, hunting around and scoffing up some sweet skirts. Beeker didn't know it yet, that the kid had busted his cherry. But Rosie knew. Cowboy'd told him what had happened in that New Neuzen whorehouse, once when Rosie was plastered on bourbon and Cowboy was high on coke. In fact, Rosie thought they should all be on vacation for the rest of time. He kept telling Beeker that all he wanted was an acre of sand on the Gulf of Mexico and enough whores to keep his hands—and whatever else—busy. Why else did they get all that money together? But no, they had to keep on hot-rodding it all around the world. Beat up this dictator. Piss on that terrorist. Drag that damsel out of the crocodile's mouth.

Playacting a bunch of fools, that's what they were doing. Men their age, not one of them under thirty-five and too many of them pushing forty, should be sitting home on chaise longues and drinking beer while they watched the goddamn VistaVision television and audiophone combination sets. Vietnam was years ago. It was years ago that they had gone out to save the world.

*Shit.*

Rosie had been in the United States Army. A Ranger. One of the real bad guys. He remembered when he and his buddies first got there. They were green. But they were ready to march north and cut off Ho Chi Minh's pecker all by themselves. They were sure they could do it and still have the time left in the day to go fishing, if Vietnamese fish bit in the afternoon. Wrong. Very, very wrong.

They all learned that in the stinking jungles of that place. Goddamn, man, that was just the most brutal shit Rosie had ever known.

So, had he been a smart man? Found a way out? Taken enough drugs like the other bros to get them through with an honorable discharge? Oh, no. Not Roosevelt Boone. No, sir.

He was *so* smart he went to his captain and begged for more training even when he knew that it would mean that his stay in that asshole of a country in the black bottom of a continent would be indefinitely prolonged. Smart move, Rosie, real smart.

Those memories all called for more bourbon than was left in his glass. "Honey, you do this some more for me?" The stewardess had a nice color to her, sort of honey brown, just enough to set off her sparkling white teeth. Just enough to make Rosie think about how lovely her behind would be if it was all that same color. Goddamn very lovely, that's how much.

He smiled at her as she poured. "No, no, sweetheart, we gotta have more than that to get us all the way to Huasteca. Come on, sweet thing, fill me up." She hesitated, looked around to see if anyone noticed how Rosie was asking her to break the rules that stipulated only a couple of ounces of alcohol be poured at once. Then she went ahead.

"Great. That's a nice girl. Now, honey, you going to be staying long in Huasteca?"

She was startled. Of course she was approached by at least one man on every flight, but she hadn't expected it of this one. He was so large and that strange earring he wore—a white skull pierced directly into his lobe—had made him seem so alien that she was not prepared for his question. "No . . . no, I have to go back to New Orleans."

"Maybe you got a sister then? One as pretty as you."

"No, no sister." It was her second lie. She didn't understand why she was doing it and she immediately regretted both statements. There was something forbidding about this big man with ebony skin and smooth talk, but there was something very attractive as well. The way a Venus flytrap is attractive, pretty enough to draw in the insect and then close its petals so quickly that the little thing doesn't discover that it's trapped until it's too late.

Women often thought that about Rosie. He was as much of a challenge as most of them ever received. This huge man, positively smelling of danger, carried with him all the possibilities of overwhelming lust and all the dangers of great destruction. Women could sense that. The stewardess did. Rosie was used to the reaction and didn't bother her anymore when she moved quickly down the aisle away from him. He especially didn't bother when she looked back once more with an expression that clearly showed her conflicted mind. Maybe she wasn't ready for the destruction of her soul today, that was all. Woman didn't want Rosie, Rosie didn't want the woman. That's all there was to it.

What the hell. He got his bourbon anyway.

He sipped it and looked over Tsali's shoulder at the big reference book on San Sebastian that the kid was reading. Smart little kid, Tsali was. Doing this thing right, did everything right. Going some place, read about it. Getting ready to fight, prepare for it.

Seventeen years old and Beeker was letting the kid be used as a front for the team. Rosie wondered if Beeker was losing it to Delilah. Had she really gotten to the team leader so much that Beeker wasn't using the sense God gave him? Hell, Tsali didn't need to go on shit like this. No way. He could sit at home and play with all those computer games that Cowboy had stuck away where Billy Leaps wouldn't find them.

Damn Beeker! There he was, thinking the kid's mind was going to rot and his body was going to wilt if he played video games, and then turning around and sending him into a country that was slated for revolution. Here's the ticket kid, and here's a rifle, but stay the hell away from those damn machines!

Seventeen. Now wait a minute, Rosie thought. What's so hot shit about seventeen? By the time Roosevelt Boone was fourteen he'd already killed his first man—a pimp who tried to turn Rosie's mother out as a whore in Newark. His mama was not going to be a whore and Rosie proved it to that man the only way he would listen to, with a knife in his forehead, right between the eyes.

That had been his first blood.

By seventeen? There'd been a rumble with another gang when Rosie shot the enemy's leader in the heart. Then there was the time a burglar tried to clean the cash register at the corner store where Rosie worked. Now, if Rosie had let the man do that, then Mr. Schuetz wouldn't have been able to pay Rosie his salary that week and Rosie needed that money to pay for his school books. There was only one way out of the dilemma so far as Rosie was concerned, and that's the way Rosie went. He took two cans down from the shelf—one can of chili and one can of baked beans—and with one in each hand, he cracked the man's skull open. *My*, that was messy.

Rosie took another big swig of bourbon to clean away the bad taste the memories had conjured up. That ghetto had been *hard*. Real hard. Heroin and gangs and rip-off ministers and fucked-up revolutionaries.

*Revolutionaries!* A bunch of assholes who proclaimed themselves the saviors of the ghetto. Most of them had learned the name Marx in prison cells. They weren't half the fools they pretended to be. They could get a whole neighborhood hopped up and ready for the revolution. *Take it to the streets!* Where on the streets? To the big houses of the slumlords who bled the ghetto dry and bought big cars with money that should have provided heat for little black babies that would die of exposure in the winter? Oh, no. Don't take it to *them*.

Then to the corrupt police officers who took payoffs from pimps and dealers and turned their heads when an honest citizen made an honest complaint about being hassled? Oh, no, not to them either. Then to the men who thought nothing of fathering children in a night—or twenty minutes, anyway—of ecstasy, but then left them to drown in poverty when the mothers couldn't bring home a paycheck big enough to insure an uninterrupted supply of Thunderbird? Hell, no, don't bring it to them—those were the revolutionaries themselves.

Take it to the streets and burn the houses where welfare mothers struggled to raise children. Break down the doors of the local liquor store and rob the man trying to build up a small business he could call his own. Tear open the shutters on a corner store where an old couple had invested their last penny and had always treated their customers fairly. Do all that and let your leaders loot the targets, move their big vans in and take out their booty, let them go around the next day and force protection money against the next "act of revolution." Rosie had seen all that and more. That was the Third World in the United States so far as Roosevelt Boone was concerned.

It made him burn.

"You listen to me, Tsali!" he cried loudly, turned suddenly on the boy. "You don't listen to any of the Third World shit they're going to feed you down here. You remember, we wouldn't have nothing to do with this crap if it wasn't an assignment. You understand? Nothing. There are good whites and bad whites, decent blacks and rotten ones, there are red men you can trust with your life and there are red men who ought to be shot on sight. You hear me, boy? You understand?"

Tsali nodded once. Didn't need a book to learn that.

# 9

After they'd unpacked, Rosie decided they should go down and look around the place. He might as well get some more bourbon in his gut, since the next day they were going to start training and it just wouldn't be fair to expect the kid to go through all that shit when Rosie was goofing off.

Like most coaches. Maybe he should just piss off. Then that part of their disguise would be authentic as well.

They took the elevator down to the lobby. The Hacienda Taninul was an old building, constructed in the traditional Spanish colonial architecture of a time gone by. The outer walls were adobe. There were many arches, a legacy of the Moslem influence on Spanish culture that had been transferred to the New World by the conquistadors. That legacy was highly appropriate, for the style was perfect for the hottest climates. Huasteca reminded Rosie of 'Nam. Hot, humid, so humid that the rain that fell that afternoon didn't bring any relief. There had already been that much moisture in the air to begin with. Whether it came down in drops of rain or just hung there didn't make much difference.

It was the kind of tropical humidity that promoted rot on

the skin, clothes, and shoe leather, creating a wet landscape suitable for the spores that sprouted and spread with such rapidity. You could get jock rot so quickly in a place like this that it'd take a case of talcum powder a day to give you some protection, and that wouldn't always be enough.

It was so hot you couldn't even tell if you were sweating. The liquid on your skin could have come from the atmosphere or your own body, and probably it had come from both. The main thing, the thing you never forgot was that the moisture was going to stay there and there wasn't a damn thing you could do about it.

"It'll be hell to run a ten-K in this weather."

Tsali shrugged at Rosie's offhand concern. The boy was harboring his dream, keeping it totally to himself. He hoped, too, that the weather wouldn't prove much of a hindrance to his training. He knew that he was there as a cover for Rosie and the other Berets when they arrived. They had given him an assignment. He had every intention of doing his part. But there was a thrill to this cover story.

Tsali had never really been able to spend time with boys his own age. He had seldom been in one place long enough to get to know any of them well, and there had been few willing to spend time with a mute full-breed anyway. He had never tested his body against his peers'. He had trained for over a year now. His muscles had swelled and strengthened with the hard work. His skills had sharpened. But the training had been with his father, a much older man, whose goals were different and entirely practical.

Now he was to have the opportunity of running a major race with kids his own age. Tsali was thrilled to think about that. A little frightened too. He was so used to rejection from other boys that he assumed that it would occur again. But now? He was an accepted member of the Black Berets. He had received more training than a marine recruit.

If every seventeen-year-old in Huasteca spat at his feet, Tsali had the security of knowing that he had a family to back him up. A family of five men who accepted him totally and who in their way probably loved him. Tsali no longer cared about the other seventeen-year-olds, and that was an advantage.

And he could run.

The daily push with Billy Leaps Beeker was some of the most enjoyable time Tsali had ever spent. The wind in his hair, worn the traditional long length of the Cherokee, his body reaching, stretching at every stride, his lungs bursting for air, his heart doubling and halving its size fifty times a minute.

Since he had trained with Billy Leaps, Tsali knew he had a chance against the others. He hadn't mentioned it to anyone else and he had never challenged the others when they had talked about this mission, assuming only that Tsali would be good enough to get by, making a credible entrant.

But Tsali wanted to win. He wanted a gold ribbon to start his own collection of medals and awards, like the one he knew his father kept hidden in a drawer in his room.

So while Rosie found the bar of the hotel, Tsali went running. Through the streets of Huasteca, narrow but surprisingly clean, spread over with banners and flags of participating nations, with bands in the tiny squares and the sound of organ music pouring through the open doors of the churches he passed.

Rosie had told him he should take a day off, but Tsali wrote: *This way I'll get to know the city.* Which wasn't a bad idea, thought Rosie, if the kid can take the heat.

# 10

Senator Mark Holden scanned the audience in the hearing room. The usual journalists and lobbyists. The other members of his Committee on Central American Relations were dozing off or else reading the newspapers or conferring with their aides about other, more important meetings scheduled for later in the day. At least some of them showed up this time. Often Holden was left to the lonely task of listening to expert testimony by himself.

It used to bother him. It bothered him until he realized that most of the men and women who came before a Senate committee didn't give a good damn whether or not there were any legislators there. They only cared about the TV cameras and the radio microphones.

The business of running the country was slowly slipping away from the politicians and being taken up by the media. It was obvious to Holden and to most others who cared. It was an irresistible phenomenon, a slow, steady progression that was making it more and more difficult for a decent man to help establish policy that had any principled, ethical base. Policy was becoming something that was determined by Mr. Neilson's ratings and Mr. Harris's polls.

Victorio Salazar, today's witness, was a man from the old school who would never understand that transition. He would ignore it to his dying day. Holden felt uneasy all of a sudden. Salazar's presence here seemed a personal challenge to him.

So far as his peers and the voters in his district were concerned, Mark Holden was of the old school himself. He'd carried his office and his principles with a consistency that had recently become rare in this country. But when Holden compared himself to Salazar, the president of San Sebastian, the senator knew there were too many compromises he'd made, too many issues he'd dodged, too many instances where he hadn't championed the right for the simple reason that it was the unpopular side of the cause.

There was a big difference between being one of the most principled men in the world and being one of the least unprincipled men in American politics. Holden wasn't proud of himself. He would have liked to tell his grandchildren more than that, relatively speaking, he hadn't been bad.

Holden knew how these things went. At this moment in history, Salazar was ignored—it was even a wonder that his own countrymen respected him as much as they did. But as soon as he was dead, or deposed, or simply gave up the never-ending battle, then the United States would declare fervently that they had lost a friend whose like might never rise again in Central America. In the meantime, however, the Committee on Central American Relations dozed and read its newspapers and conferred with its aides.

El Presidente's hair was black with thick streaks of white through it. Holden wondered if the man dyed it those brilliantly contrasting colors, or whether it was natural—then he realized that the very question showed just how much he'd been corrupted by the media. The media cared about things like that rather than about what the man had done, what the man perceived, what the man intended to do with his small, happy, frightened nation.

There was still plenty of pride in the ramrod-stiff posture of the man. He kept his face set in that fashion, as if he were forever posing for a monumental sculpture. The traces of native blood hardened some of the lines of his silhouette, itself already noble with the genes of the conquistadors.

"We're pleased to welcome our guest, the Honorable Victorio Salazar." As soon as Holden spoke into the microphones, the cameramen had turned on their blinding lights. Cameras clicked and the motor drives whirred.

The honorable senator from South Dakota put down his newspaper hurriedly and consulted a sheaf of notes that didn't exist.

The honorable senator from Arizona smiled an indulgent, condescending smile of welcome to the president of San Sebastian. The honorable senator from Arizona was under investigation for taking bribes, but he hadn't yet been convicted.

The honorable senator from Maryland straightened the bow on the front of her dress and whispered a few last words to her two aides before she sent them scurrying.

"I am grateful for the opportunity to speak to the American Senate," Salazar said. "I am grateful that your schedules permitted it."

Holden sat back. There was nothing he could say into the microphone in response to that. They all knew it, the other members of the committee and the reporters too. Salazar had been snubbed left and right in the capital. The President was at Camp David, the Secretary of State was in the Caribbean—on vacation—the Speaker of the House didn't have enough Hispanic voters in his district to give a damn about one more visiting Latin official.

It had taken every chip Holden had even to garner a respectable number of committee members for this hearing. The difficulty was to be expected. There was no trouble in San Sebastian. No American troops had been killed there within the last five administrations. No one had proof, reports, or even rumors of the presence of Cuban troops there. No major American investments endangered by local strikes. No suspicious Russians involved in "technological assistance."

Salazar had come to give a friendly warning—as a man announces to those who live nearby that there's an arsonist loose in the neighborhood. He anticipated trouble in San Sebastian, but he couldn't provide more evidence than that of a bomb here, a bank robbery there, a random killing on the beach. Given the way the rest of Central America was seething with unspeakable horrors—unspeakable except on the six o'clock news—no one was going to get upset by the minor problems of San Sebastian.

He should get some nuns killed, thought Holden. That would perk up the press. That, or have a hospital bombed, preferably one with Italian nurses. That was nearly as good as nuns to the American press who thought that all Italian nurses were nuns. Maybe have somebody plant a bomb on a school bus. The press loved that. Once he got on the front pages, then Salazar would get his aid.

Three helicopters, two hundred American troops, five new airfields, a massive inflation problem, and five thousand right- and left-wing troublemakers who invariably throng to such a scene.

"Mr. Salazar," said Senator Holden, "you are the longest-lasting political leader in the entire Western Hemisphere, and have seen regimes both north and south of you come and go. The Committee—and I'm sure the press and the American public—would be very interested to receive the benefit of your impressions of the situation in Central America."

Hell, C-Span was doing the child abuse hearings today. A case of suspected uncle-niece incest on Michigan's northern peninsula was going to get more coverage than the future of more than three hundred million people living in Mexico and Central America.

But, Holden thought, might as well let the man do it right.

The answer was long, well thought out, and wouldn't be mentioned in the next day's newspapers since Salazar didn't have a single punchy quote in the entire statement. Instead he presented a thorough, interesting, and provocative analysis of the results of the decades of violence, revolution, international interference, war, and economic exploitation on the region.

The region had become a battleground for forces that had no business there. It was a funny-shaped board on which bigger nations played dangerous games. Multinationals had private armies to protect investments. Americans supplied forces that fought against French backed regimes. Russians sent "advisors" to lead campaigns against American-supported governments. The British held onto an ancient colonial enclave for their pride and their balance of payments. And the Cubans invaded the British enclave in order to keep their citizens' minds off the disastrous economic problems of the Marxist island.

It was only natural that so much unrest was beginning to infect San Sebastian—it was a wonder that the country hadn't succumbed before now. Despite his worry, however, Salazar spoke with a kind of impassioned levelheadedness. No mean feat, that, thought Holden. He didn't blame Castro or the Russians, he didn't blame the United States for not protecting him. That's a mistake, Holden thought. The senator turned to look at one of his colleagues, Dan Maston from South Dakota. If Salazar would only claim that it was all the Cubans' fault—that the Cubans had poisoned the water and painted the hammer-and-sickle on the sides of the buses—then Maston would have sent the South Dakota National Guard if the U.S. Army wouldn't go. But the water could be drunk, and the buses were clean, and Salazar was above the jingoism that would blame an enemy for sins it hadn't committed.

On the other hand, Salazar didn't protest that American corporations had vitiated the San Sebastian economy and that the lack of American assistance had kept his people in ignorance and poverty, and therefore nobody could read and all the children had measles. A little bit of that might have gone a long way toward enlisting the help of the senator from Maryland, who once a month proclaimed that the first goal of the United States Congress ought to be the eradication of all childhood illnesses.

Then, at last, Salazar's goal was revealed. Holden had expected it all along, but he hadn't expected the San Sebastian president to be so bluntly honest in even this. "I suggest that the United States, the Soviet Union, and their respective allies remove themselves from Central America. I suggest that all the nations of the region sign a nonaggression pact with the American and Soviet governments as the guarantees."

Dead silence, except for two lethargic clicks of somebody's camera.

Maston started to speak, but Maston's South Dakota speech was slow and drawling, and Holden beat him to the punch.

"Thank you, Mr. Salazar, for your very interesting and informative presentation. It would be a great shame if the leaders of this nation and all the members of Congress did not ponder well these insights you've provided us all today. This session of the committee is hereby adjourned."

After he'd banged the gavel, Holden sat back in his chair. The cameras were off now. He could light up a cigar, one of his great pleasures, but one that on television looked pompous and fat-catty.

The placidity of the press corps as it gathered up its equipment measured Salazar's unimportance in their eyes. No one rushed up to him with frantic follow-up questions, no one begged for an interview or even an elaboration. They'd evidently even got enough pictures of him. One would have been enough, since no picture was going to run anyway. They all probably wished they'd been assigned to the uncle-niece incest business.

Maston and the other senators were up and out, without a word or a nod or a smile either to Salazar or to Holden. They were, in fact, pretty pissed off.

If Salazar had caused a ruckus of some sort, each of them might have gotten a few precious seconds on the nightly news, maybe even an invitation to spend a couple of minutes on the CBS Morning News. Those seconds and minutes tallied voter recognition and, ultimately, votes. But Salazar's speech had been a big zero. A blank.

Holden watched the whole thing break up. He was pleasantly surprised when one woman finally did go up to Salazar. There was no good reason for a woman that beautiful to be there unless she was media. Holden couldn't place her though. That was surprising; he thought he knew them all by now. She was short, and that always threw you off. He remembered the first time he'd been interviewed behind a desk on a national news show. The moderator was sitting on a telephone book.

Who was she? Blond, with an incredible body. Jesus, what a body! And the way she walked! It was only when the tall, dark-skinned man walked up beside her and Salazar that Holden realized they probably weren't with the press at all. They just didn't read for press.

Fine figure of a man, that one. He stood with his legs slightly apart, his hands joined behind his back. He must have been a marine at some time. No one else would so automatically assume parade rest in civilian life. He hadn't lost his training either. Holden unconsciously patted his own stomach, bloated with the deposits of fat that came from a life lived behind a desk. This man made him aware of his physical deficiencies as much as Salazar had underscored his moral limitations.

What a rotten day.

# 11

Delilah and Beeker flanked President Salazar as he left the Senate hearing chamber. The president was obviously disappointed and distressed with his reception. "Not a single word from any of them, senators or press. Nothing!"

It wasn't his pride that was hurt. It was the sense of futility that got to him. Maybe he just wouldn't bother with the United States anymore. Let it fall through willful ignorance.

Delilah didn't protest or try to defend the senators and press. Salazar just didn't understand that he was too much in the middle of the road. If he'd attacked from either the left or the right, there would have been some response. If from the right, certain of the politicians would have flocked round him. If from the left, he'd have been supported by the many members of the American press corps who had long ago given up hiding their own pro-left tendencies. If the San Sebastian president had only attacked the United States—or Cuba—and blamed it for his country's problems, he would have had plenty of attention.

Beeker just kept walking. So far as he was concerned the guy should be happy no one paid attention to him. Who wants that kind of bullshit as part of his life? Damn reporters climbing all over a man's privacy, that wasn't worth shit. Salazar should be damned pleased he'd escaped.

They went down the wide shallow steps of the Capitol. "Do you have a car coming for you?" Delilah asked.

"There it is," Salazar responded. An ancient Cadillac limousine with small flags of San Sebastian on either side of its hood was parked over to the side of the oval driveway in front of the building. The driver, seeing the president, got out of the car and stood at respectful attention, but Salazar shook his head and waved the driver on. "I'd rather walk."

Billy Leaps glanced at Delilah, who shrugged. Maybe the walk would dissipate a little of his frustration.

They turned to the right and started in a generally northwesterly direction.

Schoolchildren by the busload, families by the station-wagon load, foreign visitors by the planeload, all of them descended on the District of Columbia to view the museums, see the workings of the government, trudge through the historic buildings that really seemed to have so little to do with them.

This was the height of the season. The cherry blossoms had bloomed just a week before. Now the petals were scattered over the shorn lawns, and there was already a hint of the nasty summer that would follow. The Mall and the streets that led toward it were packed, not only with the traffic of government workers, but with the rambling tour groups herded on by bored and exasperated guides. As soon as a street became free of the restraints imposed by the National Park Service, it became jammed with hot-dog stands, granola stands, taco stands, ice-cream stands, and more, all serving up enormous quantities of food that looked a great deal better on the stick, or in the cup, or in someone else's hands than it tasted in one's own mouth.

And if the stands didn't take up enough room on the sidewalks, there were the street performers to make it nearly impossible to walk. Jugglers, zither players, even a string quartet were crowded into tiny spaces and made noise and created little knots of congestion around them. Mimes in white face, with vaguely clownlike costumes, had a little trick of picking a person out of the hustling crowd and walking behind him or her, imitating his walk precisely—showing just how ridiculous the posture and gait and rhythm of a human being in motion could be.

One mime slipped in right behind Salazar in the crowd and began to imitate the president's proud, angered, hurried step. Salazar had been injured in the defense of his country thirty years before and walked now with a slight limp. The mime captured this too, and the effect on the thin performer in the sad-eyed makeup was patently ridiculous. The crowd noticed, and pointed, and laughed, and Salazar—momentarily drawn back to the present out of his thoughts—began to look around in astonishment.

Beeker was angry, and was just about to break someone's arm, but Delilah was there before him. In a gesture that looked simply as if she'd stumbled, she planted the spike heel of her shoe squarely onto the mime's soft-shod foot.

The mime yelped, dropped his impersonation of Salazar, and hopped off to one side in pain.

"What is it?" said Salazar, turning suspiciously.

"Nothing at all, Mr. President," said Delilah, with a smile.

As they proceeded, the light and festive air of the mingling crowds and the colorful vendors seemed to take the edge off Salazar—or perhaps it was just some internal process of recovery that was working on him. Beeker had hope that Salazar would give in soon and opt for the protection of the limousine that was following them as best it could in the noontime traffic.

Delilah seemed to read Beeker's thoughts—he was made

nervous by the density of the crowd. It was one thing to protect a man in a hotel room or an embassy, and another on the street when Salazar obviously didn't *need* to be on the street.

"Mr. President—" she ventured.

He nodded with an understanding smile. "I understand," he said. "Call the limousine."

Beeker went to the curb, raised his arm once, and got a responding wave from the limousine driver, who was stuck at the red light on the previous block, caught behind an out-of-state driver intent on taking an illegal and probably impossible left turn.

Billy Leaps, Delilah, and Salazar crossed the street with the light and waited on the opposite curb for the limousine to maneuver toward them.

On this side of the street a small puppet theater had been set up, giving the old Punch and Judy show, with Punch first hurling his infant out of the window and then beating Judy over the head with a stick when she protested his unfatherly behavior.

A number of children had gathered round and were laughing and pointing, and a number of adults stood about, scandalized by the violence of the piece. Salazar began to watch, amused.

Then even Delilah was entranced for a few moments, laughing when the devil rose up out of hell and dragged down Punch as punishment for the murder of his wife. It really was very funny.

A horn blew behind her, and she turned. There was the San Sebastian limousine.

"Mr. President," she said, placing a hand on Salazar's arm. He turned with a grin.

A shot was fired.

Instinctively Delilah dropped to the ground, pulling hard on Salazar's arm as she did so. He was close behind her. The children and adults all around them screamed.

And where was Beeker?

Delilah looked all around and saw nothing but that the puppet theater—a tall, narrow box with the stage about four feet off the ground and curtains below—was in violent motion, rocking from side to side.

Then there was a scream, like Punch's scream when he's dragged off to hell—but this one was real.

There was a difference, and Delilah knew it.

Adults were trying to drag their children away, but the children—despite the gunshot, which had apparently hit no one—were entranced.

Then the puppet theater was still again, ominously still.

The skirt beneath the tiny stage parted, and a tall, dark-skinned man slipped out. The front of his suit jacket, his shirt, and his trousers were stained with bright-red blood. He held Punch convulsing in his right hand.

He was like the devil out of Punch's hell, come real to drag a few children away with him.

Everyone screamed and scattered.

In the distance came the shrill blast of a policeman's whistle.

Delilah already had the limousine door open, and Salazar was climbing inside. In another moment Delilah and Beeker were in as well.

The limousine took off.

With a vague air of distaste, Delilah said, "I don't like street performers any better than you do, but—"

Beeker held out the Punch puppet. Delilah looked at it thoughtfully and then plucked it softly from the barrel of the revolver that it was hiding.

Beeker held out the weapon for her to examine. "A CZ seventy-five," he said. "It's Czech."

# 12

Delilah's magic usually worked. It just took a little more time this once. After all, a killing that took place so near the Capitol, on the edge of government property, with forty children and ten adults as witnesses—even if the escape was made in a consular vehicle—wasn't that easily contained. The District Attorney's Office of the District of Columbia had insisted on questioning Beeker.

Delilah refused.

"Hell you say," said the assistant district attorney who'd been assigned to the case.

He and Delilah and Beeker met in one of the small interrogation rooms of the police headquarters of the District of Columbia.

Beeker sat silently by, unconcerned and bored, as Delilah related the story. It was more or less an account of what had happened.

The assistant D.A. stared at her, amazed. "There's a man dead—very dead, I might add; I saw the corpse myself—and here's a man who admits he did it, and you can't just sit there and tell me to fill out the forms and file them."

"No," Delilah admitted, "but maybe someone else can." She checked her watch, shrugged, and said, "He's late."

"Who's late?" asked the assistant district attorney, glancing uneasily at Beeker, who was leafing through a sports magazine he'd found on the floor underneath his chair.

The telephone buzzed.

"It's for you," said Delilah.

The assistant D.A. picked up the telephone, listened for a few moments as amazement and terror gathered on his face, and said, "Yes, sir" twice. Then he handed the receiver to Delilah. "He wants to talk to you."

Delilah spoke into the receiver. "No, sir," she said. "I don't imagine there'll be any trouble." She looked at the assistant district attorney, who shook his head vehemently. "No," she confirmed, "there won't be any trouble. And I apologize for—"

She listened for a few moments, said, "I will," and hung up.

She smiled at the assistant D.A., who got up hurriedly and left the room.

"Who was that on the phone?" Beeker asked.

Delilah smiled.

The embassy of the Republic of San Sebastian was in the cluster of such buildings along Massachusetts Avenue in the northwest quadrant of the District of Columbia. It was a gracious area, and the old mansions that in another city would have been torn down or turned into undertaking establishments here survived because of their utility as ambassadors' residences.

San Sebastian had bought its own building nearly seventy years before. It was a graceful and impressive Victorian mansion, a building of such proportions that the poor nation couldn't possibly have afforded it at today's market prices.

Beeker and Delilah arrived at the front door and were immediately ushered into the main reception room. The guard left them and in only a short time President Salazar entered from a side door. “A drink? Please. After all, you have apparently saved my life.”

Beeker didn’t like that little qualifier “apparently.” Damn right he’d saved the guy’s life.

“I imagine that the puppeteer was waiting for your limousine to pass,” said Delilah. “I think that Mr. Beeker really did save your life, Mr. President.”

“Thank you,” said the president politely to Billy Leaps. “Now the drink?”

“White wine for me,” said Delilah. “Mr. Beeker won’t have anything this early in the day.”

Beeker retreated to a small chair in the corner of the room. He hated pretentious houses like this. He knew that the embassy was done in what Delilah would call “the best possible taste,” but that didn’t help matters so far as he was concerned.

The room was full of little *things*. Statues to break, tables to knock over, rugs to soil, *things*. Any kid that walked in there would have a hell of a time. So would any real man.

This was a woman’s room so far as Beeker was concerned. The kind of place where you don’t put up your feet and you don’t have a beer in case you might put it down on the table that was too precious to use as a table.

Beeker hated the idea of things that weren’t supposed to be used. Why the fuck have them then? Sure, he knew it was a fake room anyway, just a public space to throw parties where lots of people who thought they were important could stand around and swill booze that was too expensive to get drunk on, except that they did. He knew that game.

His displeasure was right there on his face. Anyone could see it. President Salazar misread it. “You must not feel badly about that man.”

Beeker looked at the statesman in disbelief. *Sorry about that man?* Then he turned his gaze on Delilah, as if to say, You deal with this.

Delilah looked close to laughter, and she cleared her throat, looked away from Beeker, and said, "Mr. President, you must understand. Mr. Beeker is a veteran of the Vietnam War, and since then he's had considerable experience in the . . . security field. I know for a fact that he didn't particularly *enjoy* this afternoon's events, but I don't think they've scarred him. He's ready to go forward with his commitment to protect you from future outrages."

Salazar looked at Beeker again, displeasure in his face now. That was fine by Billy Leaps. He was just doing his job and didn't need approval from this guy . . . or anyone else.

All he wanted out of the job was the satisfaction of having done it right and the two hundred acres of empty forest that Delilah had promised him.

"As Mr. Beeker pointed out in the car, Mr. President, the weapon used by the assassin was Czech in origin."

Salazar shrugged, as if to say what both Billy Leaps and Delilah knew—that weapons were not respectors of international boundaries. Czech guns showed up everywhere, as did Soviet arms, and American arms, and French arms, and so on. Because the puppeteer had carried a Czech sidearm was no reason to suppose he had ever been to Prague.

"There was also a note on the body. It was written in Cyrillic characters, but interestingly, it wasn't Russian. It was Bulgarian."

That was more trustworthy evidence, and Salazar's brow wrinkled. "Why would the Bulgarians be after me? *Any* Bulgarians?"

Beeker took out the sports magazine he had brought from the police station and opened it up to the prediction of winning football teams for the season two years back. He'd decided that he didn't care for heads of state, even those who were being hunted down by Bulgarians posing as puppeteers.

"Often," said Delilah, "when the Soviets are interested in placing some distance between themselves and certain . . . operations, they use Bulgarians. They have, for some time, been some of the most effective operatives the Soviets have. There's a certain . . . barbarism . . . to the Bulgarian, which comes in handy."

"Russian agents will perform any barbarity," said Salazar dryly.

"Yes," admitted Delilah, "but they'll hesitate a moment, and the Bulgarians won't."

"But why me? *Bulgarians?*"

"Why isn't the question right now. Where and when and how are the questions. The message found on the operative was in code, but the code was known. There's a backup, and it will be put into effect while you're still here in Washington."

"I have no intention of fleeing from *Bulgarians*," said the president of San Sebastian, and then he added something beneath his breath, in Spanish.

"We don't want you to leave," said Delilah, glancing at Beeker and frowning at the magazine. "We want you to stay right here. We intend to use you as bait to capture whoever is involved."

"Bait?" Salazar looked uncomfortable.

"Perhaps that's too strong a word," said Delilah, but then she couldn't think of any other.

# 13

The razor hit the mirror with quick, expert strokes.

*Click. Click. Click.*

Music to Cowboy's ears. Just the finest symphonic sound he could ever imagine. In front of him the sight that provided an equivalent amount of visual pleasure.

A mound of cocaine. Two grams. The best that was to be had in Louisiana. Rosie had introduced him to a guy named Sambo—honest to God, a black guy who called himself Sambo—and Sambo gave Cowboy his telephone number, and last time Cowboy was in New Orleans he'd called up Sambo. Sambo didn't live there anymore, but Sambo's sister did, and Sambo's sister was this crippled girl, and this crippled girl—Cowboy never did find out her name—sold the best cocaine that was to be had in New Orleans, in Louisiana, and in the whole damn eleven states of Dixie. Maybe she was saving up for an operation.

Cowboy felt guilty about the transaction. Not because it was illegal, which it certainly was. Not because he knew cocaine was bad for him, which it probably was. But because Billy Leaps Beeker didn't approve of cocaine.

Cowboy'd hidden it. Inside a sock inside another sock at the back of the bottom drawer of the dresser in his room. Waiting for a time when he'd be all alone, or just alone with Rosie. Rosie didn't care about cocaine, for some reason. But Cowboy couldn't do it in front of Tsali, or Harry or Marty. Marty'd tell, for one thing. Marty was like that. Not like a tattle, but it would slip out somehow, and Beeker'd come down hard.

But here he was alone. Harry and Marty were off in Nevada. Goddamn Nevada. Beeker was up in D.C. planking Delilah. Goddamn Washington fucking Capitol Hill. Rosie and Tsali were in some godforsaken Latin country running goddamn races with the Arabs and the Abos . . .

Goddamn Latin country!

He was like a teenager waiting till his mommy and daddy left home so he could pull out the magazines and jerk off.

Yeah, that's what this was like.

Cowboy took out a very new, very crisp hundred-dollar bill that he always kept in his wallet for just such a time as this. He rolled it into a tight tube. He leaned over, inserted one end of the bill into his left nostril, and put the other at the end of one of the four lines of white powder. He breathed in and moved the tube down the line. He lifted it and looked to see if he'd need to go back. But no, he'd gotten every crumb.

The cocaine flooded half his nose.

He did a second line, using his right nostril.

He wet his middle finger, wiped up the haze that remained on the mirror, and rubbed it against his gums.

Goddamn, why didn't dentists use *that* instead of novocaine?

He sat back and let the drug take its course.

He was flooded with good feeling.

Goddamn Latin country . . .

Latin ladies . . .

If there was anything that Cowboy loved the way he loved cocaine, it was Latin ladies. Beautiful women with fine smooth skin, lovely accented voices, and willing dispositions. Cowboy loved them so much that he had married several of them. He hadn't divorced them because Latin ladies were Catholic and didn't believe in divorce. Which was fine, because that was the way things were, and right now Cowboy didn't see anything wrong with the way things were.

He liked the courtship, the romance, the weddings, the bridal dinners, and especially the honeymoons. It didn't even bother him when a young Latin lady held him off till the honeymoon. He could wait.

It was difficult sometimes. Fathers and brothers and cousins of Latin ladies tended to take a dim view of Cowboy's abandoning his wife. Latin men were into revenge the way American men were into televised football. What they didn't understand was that Cowboy's motives were always pure. What more did any Latin lady want than marriage and a honeymoon with a rich, handsome, romantic American pilot? She could feast the rest of her life on the memories that Cowboy built, and she wouldn't have to put up with the inconvenience of a husband.

Cowboy had intended to save the other two lines he'd drawn for later. But they looked ripe for the plundering. So he plundered them. One after the other. Who knew when he'd be alone in the house again, and it had been so *long*.

Mother C would put him in a good mood for tomorrow's work.

If he could remember what that was supposed to be.

Oh right, upgrading the surveillance system. For somebody who declared his mistrust in modern machinery and mechanics twenty-five times a day, Billy Leaps Beeker was pretty hot to trot with his commands to Cowboy on keeping the silent sentries in operation.

Thank God that this last piece of property Billy Leaps had bought was separate from the rest. Nothing but a forest and a couple of sinkholes. Nothing to protect there, but if Billy Leaps ever heard of poachers on that few hundred acres, then Cowboy knew he was going to be sent out there with his wire and his infrared cameras and his expert knowledge. And if Beeker got more land, if he brought it all together into one large ranch, there'd be something over one thousand acres then. Every square of inch needing constant patrolling by camera and sensors. Great. Cowboy could do it. With enough cocaine he could do it. With enough cocaine Cowboy could do just about anything. Not just about. *Any* fucking thing. He—

The telephone rang.

He picked it up and hadn't even said hello before the voice started telling him a story. "Cowboy, I got this redhead, you wouldn't believe her, you wouldn't believe what she can do. She's got this trick, see, she—"

"I don't want to hear about it, Marty," said Cowboy genially, and hung up.

He wandered away, back in the direction of the kitchen. He'd give it an hour maybe, then break out another half gram. Just to build on. Who knew when he'd get it again. He—

The telephone rang again.

Should have expected that, he thought to himself, as he pulled a beer from the refrigerator. He jerked off the tab and took a long swallow. Beer always tasted like something else when it mixed with cocaine at the back of your throat. Cowboy wasn't sure what it tasted like, but it was something—

The telephone continued to ring.

"What's up?" said the voice, another voice, a slow, sad voice this time.

"Everything," said Cowboy, trying to sound as if he hadn't just ingested a couple of hundred dollars' worth of cocaine in the past ten minutes. "I'm all alone. I'm protecting three hundred acres with every part of my body. Beak's in D.C. with Delilah. Rosie and Tsali ran off." He took a sip of the beer, still not able to figure out just what it tasted like. "Went off running," he corrected himself. "Rosie and Tsali went off running in some damn place. San Sebastian. Some sort of games. Some sort—"

"You mean San Sebastian in Central America?" Harry asked.

"Yeah," said Cowboy, "some damn Latin place. Full of damn Latin ladies. None of them married to me. Never got married in San Sebastian. Been there, but I never got married there, I—"

"What are we supposed to do?" Harry asked. "Marty and me?"

"You're supposed to go down there," said Cowboy carefully, realizing that it might be apparent that he was on cocaine, even over the telephone. He tried to bring stolid boring level-headedness back into the conversation. With enough cocaine, he could do even that—appear that he wasn't on cocaine at all. "As soon as you get back here, you go down there."

"Why don't we go direct from here?" Harry asked.

Cowboy pondered this. It seemed like a great idea. If Marty and Harry went directly from Las Vegas to San Sebastian, then maybe Cowboy would have a couple of extra days to do more coke. Sounded like a great idea. But what if he ran out? Maybe Sambo's crippled sister had had her operation and could drive up there with a couple of ounces. An ounce was three and a half grams. No, wait, it was two and a half. He—

"Cowboy?" asked Harry. "You still there?"

"Go direct," said Cowboy quickly. "You got your passports?"

"Yep."

"Go direct," repeated Cowboy. "Do a good job. Tell Rosie I said hi. Come back alive and all that shit."

"Cowboy," said Harry after a moment, "are you gonna be all right?"

"Yep," said Cowboy, unintentionally imitating Harry's voice. "Yep. I'll be fine. Kill me an Abo. Chalk up a A-rab. Slice a geek. Have fun. Don't let Marty get married to any Latin ladies or I'll be jealous."

"Bye," said Harry uncertainly, and hung up in Las Vegas.

Cowboy stared at the receiver for a few moments, until the recorded announcement came on, advising him to replace it. He set it down softly on the cradle, concluding that very probably Harry hadn't noticed anything strange about his conversation. Certainly nothing that Harry was likely to attribute to a particular white and expensive powdered drug.

# 14

Rosie sat on a pier that stuck out a few dozen yards into the Gulf of Mexico, with his pole forgotten in the water, thinking, The kid can run!

They'd watched him for months back at the farm in Louisiana. No one thought to take out a stopwatch, though. He was just another teenager running a few miles in the morning with his daddy. He took it well, kept up with Beeker, and that was all. But the little bastard had had this smile on his face the first time Rosie decided to clock him on the outskirts of Huasteca. Tsali knew.

They had all thought that Tsali would simply be credible as an entry to the Third World Teenage Games. Some fake times from fake trials all put together by Delilah and he was their cover into the place. He'd been entered to the ten-kilometer race, a six and two-tenths mile contest that was laid out through the streets and suburbs of Huasteca. He'd only have to do it twice, once to pass the trials and once during the race itself. Only the first one was of any real importance, for his making a decent time would give them an excuse for remaining another five days. But even if Tsali failed that, they could still hang around without much problem.

But the kid had averaged under five minutes a mile!

He could win the goddamned thing! When was that kid going to stop astonishing them? The little fucker had known it too. That was the real kicker. You could tell that by the grin on his face when Rosie had announced the elapsed time. That day, at the kid's insistence, Rosie'd entered him into a second event. A half-marathon—thirteen point one miles—and that's what Tsali was doing right now.

*Little punk was only supposed to be a cover!*

Like all the others, Rosie knew he was soft on Tsali. The boy was the magic element that transformed the Black Berets from just a team of men who were trained to fight into something closer to a family. A group of guys couldn't really show their affection for each other. You don't go around being all sloppy about another adult male, even if he had saved your life or something else just as important. But a kid? You could use the kid to take care of that sort of thing.

They all did it. Showered him with avuncular affection. Trips, presents, time spent patiently training him in everything they knew. They gave Tsali all of it.

Not one of them felt good about his being used on this assignment. There was something sad about that, seeing him grow up so quickly. Sure, he thought everything was great. After all, before this past year with them he'd been bounced from foster home to juvenile center to God-knew-what-else all his life. What more could he ask for than to have a chance to become a full-fledged member of the team?

But they knew what they'd brought him into. Being a Black Beret wasn't all that great. Not one of them said it was. In fact, it was a pretty shitty way to live your life. The thing was, none of them had had any choice about it. They'd all tried civilian life, after 'Nam. Each one had attempted it in a different way. Jobs, marriage, apartments and houses and mortgages and cars that were always in the shop and bills that had to be put off till next month, football games on television. They had all play-acted at just being regular guys. It had been a charade. None of them had been able to make it that way.

Other veterans had made it. Come back, covered over the memories, forgiven themselves, forgiven the officers who'd betrayed them, forgot the people they'd murdered, let their strange talents rust, kissed their wives and hugged their children and wept over their parents' new graves, and said, "Oh, wow, is that what the new Chevies look like?" And of course some hadn't made it at all, but were living in caves in eastern Oregon, shooting at everything that made a noise and waxing totally mad in the light of the full moon. The Black Berets had fallen somewhere in between. They forgot nothing, they hadn't changed—the only problem was that the war had been pulled out from under them.

Rosie never had figured it all out, though he'd thought it over many times. But the bottom line was that they were Black Berets. They had to be members of a fighting team. They had to live the warrior's life. The barrackslike rooms at Beeker's farm may have appeared an unnecessary deprivation to others, but they were the most natural thing in the world to Beeker and the four men who followed him. The feel of an M-16 might be something that other men felt fairly comfortable with on a rifle range, but the M-16 was like a third arm to the Black Berets.

That was the problem with Tsali. That he was being brought into something that looked like an elite group. The optimal brotherhood. He liked the image, and he wanted to belong. Rosie understood that. But Tsali'd been blooded, he'd already had to take life in Louisiana and New Neuzen. A home changes once blood has been spilled on the threshold. Tsali was probably already accumulating psychological scars. He wasn't entering a band of charmed warriors, he was being ushered into a special circle of hell.

It made the running all the more horrible, Rosie thought. It was painful to see the kid whenever he approached anything that seemed normal. Here he was, just being a seventeen-year-old with a shot for a medal in an international track event. Rosie wanted him to have it, desperately. He wanted to let Tsali have just a single thing that was normal, that he could look back to when he was older—if he got to be older—and brag about.

Damn. He could run. Boy should be able to do that and not have to worry about international intrigue, dope smugglers, Facists, Communists, anything-ists. Just be a kid. And win a goddamn race.

Problem was the order would probably come down on high that it was Tsali's mission to kill the man who held the stop-watch. That's how things went in the Black Berets.

Rosie heard the thumping of feet on the wooden dock. He turned around and saw Tsali coming toward him. The kid's hair was plastered to his skull with sweat. He was wearing a pair of gym shorts and his track shoes. A little scrap of a shirt was twisted and filthy with sweat and dust that had turned to a stiffened mud. He ran past Rosie to the end of the pier, did a kind of theatrical wavering on the very edge, and then came back again, grinning.

Rosie's pole bobbed with every step.

"One hour seven, ten and one-tenths second," said Rosie, frowning.

Tsali signed violently.

"Don't pull none of that deaf-and-dumb shit on me," said Rosie. "I can't make it out." There was a moment when Tsali looked frustrated and upset. Then Rosie grinned. "You're too good, kid. Much too good. How you gonna take people out if you got gold medals dragging you down all the time? If this keeps up, the goddamn reporters are gonna be begging me for your photograph. And I don't have none, and your daddy would kill me if your picture ever got in a paper. So why you do this to me, Tsali? Why you run one seven ten point one on me? 'Cause you know I don't like it."

Rosie's little good-natured tirade gave Tsali the opportunity to begin to recover his breath.

He walked away again, up and down the pier, until his body grew calm. As he did, Rosie took up his knife and cut more bait. There hadn't been a nibble in more than thirty minutes, so Rosie knew what was on the hook must have been scavenged.

Tsali at last sat down cross-legged at Rosie's side.

"Go on," said Rosie, "take a swim here. And while you're down there, find whatever it is that's been gobbling my bait and give it one to the neck, will you?"

Tsali nodded, struggled to take off his shoes, peeled off the muddy shirt, and stood up, a little stiffly. He pulled up on the elastic band of his shorts and then walked out a little farther onto the pier, just to make sure he'd be diving in deep water. The waves of the Gulf were crashing in at the deserted shore no more than a few dozen yards away.

He bent his legs and then sprang forward, arms before him, and sliced perfectly into the water. Hardly a splash.

"Next thing I know he'll want to compete in the diving events too," Rosie muttered. He knew he didn't have to worry about Tsali in the water. The kid could swim like a fish. Rosie watched as Tsali swam straight out, breasting the waves easily and effortlessly. Boy could probably swim all the way to Cuba if he wanted, Rosie thought as he began to reel in again. Boy could—

"Holy shit!"

His first thought was to pick up his rifle and start firing.

But he didn't have a rifle.

Just his knife and his knife was no good.

Not with Tsali a good hundred yards beyond the pier, and between Tsali and Rosie, seven frogmen swimming in toward shore.

No, wait.

Eight frogmen.

With spearguns.

Between him and Tsali.

# 15

Rosie sat still, his mouth agape, making rapid calculations. When you've survived this long as a fighting man, you go onto automatic pilot at a time like this. Your head turns into a computer and calculates the odds, reviews the options, and churns out the scenario with the best chance of leaving you alive and everybody else dead.

The computer in his head quickly told Rosie that this time he didn't have to do a thing. He was a black man, fishing off the end of a rickety pier on a deserted stretch of beach. Nothing more natural in this part of the world. He was barefoot and wearing a pair of cut-offs. Thank God the T-shirt he was wearing was a plain one. For the previous Christmas Marty had given him a shirt imprinted with the legend:

JOIN THE RESERVES:

TRAVEL TO EXOTIC DISTANT LANDS

MEET EXCITING UNUSUAL PEOPLE AND KILL THEM

(BUT ONLY ON WEEKENDS)

Right. Just as well Rosie hadn't brought along that little article of clothing.

What were these eight men doing and where were they going? Rosie didn't know. They must have assumed that someone would see them and they couldn't have counted on opening fire as soon as they landed. Could they?

*Why don't I have a weapon?*

A weapon that fired bullets and killed frogmen from a safe distance, he meant. He did have a knife, but the odds were bad. Rosie could have run, but then they'd get to him—no two ways about it. Man runs away from you is a man smart enough to be scared of you and if he was that smart, then he already knew too much . . .

Tsali! *Oh, Christ, kid, get back!* Tsali was swimming toward shore with all the speed he could muster. The frogmen must have come in right under him and just never looked up at that moment. Oh, Jesus, what was the kid doing?

Rosie was still sitting very still, calmly reeling in his line, and watching only out of the corner of his eye, as if the last thing in the world he was aware of was the eight frogmen, with harpoon spears, paddling in toward shore. But Rosie could see not only the intruders, he could see Tsali too.

The boy was cutting through the water with great precision, making no noise, the fluttering of his feet just a minute movement in the already choppy water. He caught up to the last of the frogmen. There was a sudden movement as the shocked stranger suddenly seemed to freeze in the water. The two heads disappeared beneath the surface. In a quick moment Tsali reappeared and now had a knife in his mouth.

Holy shit! Well, if this was going to be water fighting, Rosie might as well be in the fucking water. He threw aside his reel, took his bait knife, and dived, his own big body making a significantly bigger splash than Tsali's had. He saw the look on the point frogman's face, more of a puzzled speculation than fear. The wrong thing to feel at that moment. Because Rosie's dive had taken him deep into the water and he was underneath the point man. When Rosie came up toward him, he had his knife poised to cut into the man's lungs.

The tip of the knife pierced the suit and the flesh beneath it. Rosie then dragged the blade down, slicing through the flesh. He wasn't dead yet, but he was stunned, and soon he'd be gone. Using his surprise to advantage, Rosie grabbed the speargun that was still held loosely in the man's hand, turned in the water, and fired it at the man he knew must be coming up close behind.

The man behind was very close, which meant that the spear buried very deeply into his forehead. More blood ribboned out and churned in the water.

Rosie knew that you could get only so much mileage from a surprise attack. The surprise went away. He grabbed the man with the spear in his forehead, turned him around, and employed the corpse as a shield. Just in time, for the corpse shuddered with the impact of another spear that had been meant for Rosie.

Rosie reached round and grabbed the mouthpiece off the dead man's face, and drank in the necessary oxygen. The third frogman, who had fired the spear, was closing in. Rosie moved the corpse in his hands and used it as cover to let him get closer to the new enemy. Line up, fellas . . .

The third frogman was about to close in, when Rosie suddenly pushed the corpse toward him. In a single moment of revulsion, the third frogman lost it. Because in that moment, Rosie's arm flashed out, and Rosie's knife sliced the man's oxygen hose.

Bubbles of compressed air seemed to explode out of the hose, which whipped about savagely in the water. That would have been enough to frighten any diver—the loss of his air supply—but Rosie's arm completed the circuit by ripping off the man's mask.

The man was momentarily blinded by the salt water.

Momentarily was enough time for Rosie. He backhanded the knife against the third frogman's throat.

The dying man struggled and flailed, and filled the water with blood.

Rosie took one more long suck on the hose of the corpse he was still holding, then let the dead man go. He had a few seconds—five maybe—in which he could remain hidden by the swirl of blood in the water. But even with the air in his lungs, he couldn't last long down there. He'd been psychologically unprepared for the fight—as unprepared as any Black Beret ever got—and truth to tell, he wasn't at his best under salt water with a bait knife as a weapon. Holding up the dead weight of the corpse had tired his arms. He made the decision to break the surface. It was seven or eight feet above him, rolling and green.

He shot straight up through the blood and then into the trough between two waves. His knife ready, he was ready to take on number four in a continuing series. But there wasn't any number four. He counted three more corpses. Tsali's victims. The kid's rear attack had given him an incredible boost in his odds for survival. Their oxygen tanks acting as buoys, two of Rosie's corpses now bobbed to the surface. The third one, for whatever reason, remained down below.

But that was only six. So where were—

The bullets sounded like stinging pebbles. But Rosie knew their intent and immediately dived under. He could see where they entered the water, close, much too close to him. As soon as the bullets changed from the medium of air to that of water, they slowed, altered course, and soon became harmless. But the bullets kept coming, and Rosie couldn't stay under forever.

All he could do was maneuver himself beneath another of the corpses, work the mouthpiece from the dead man's clenched teeth, and breathe for a few moments.

And pray. Pray hard.

Jesus, where was that kid?

This was the worst sort of engagement with an enemy. The opposing forces were unknown, their abilities and their verve untested. Rosie always felt better if he at least knew the nationality of the men he killed. He peered up through the water at the face of the corpse above him. Couldn't tell much except that he was Caucasian and blond—that could be just about anybody. There were other questions too. Were the survivors going to stay there and make sure that the unexpected defenders were killed? Or would they disperse, driven by the need to find shelter on land or to make a promised contact of more importance than one black man with a knife? Did they realize there were only two of them out here? And *were* there two of them? Had they taken Tsali out? Could he trust this oxygen tank? How long—

The bullets had stopped. It took him a moment to realize that. Rosie waited five minutes. A full five minutes, then raised his head out of the water on the sea side of the floating corpse.

There was only one person on the pier. Tsali. Little bastard was waving to him.

# 16

Now, Rosie said to himself, remember, you are just another incompetent track coach, that's all.

Sure he was, just another track coach who'd killed three men yesterday and the teenager he was coaching killed three himself. Wasn't this the way it always went? Sure it was.

It had been Rosie's first thought, as he peered over the corpse in the water, that Tsali had managed to take out the last two as well, but that hadn't been the case. The two survivors had given up and raced off down the beach toward the little fishing village where Rosie and Tsali had come for the day. When Rosie swam in, he dragged the corpse along with him, pulled open his suit searching for belongings or identification—but he found nothing.

It was Tsali who pointed to the instructions on the oxygen tank—small-lettered, and concise, and printed in the Cyrillic alphabet.

Now, less than eighteen hours later, they were standing in the national stadium of San Sebastian, which had been specially refurbished for the meet. It wasn't the biggest they'd ever seen—about the size of a high-school football stadium in Texas—but

Rosie knew that when it was filled with cheering fans, it'd be more than big enough. Big enough for the frogmen who'd survived to take aim and fire and put a bullet in Rosie's head. Rosie knew the two must have had a pressing assignment to just leave their buddies floating in the water, dead or dying. If they were the real soldiers Rosie thought they were, they'd want to make up for the destruction of their small invasion force.

It was just after dawn. There were only a few hardy kids out in the center of the oval track practicing the shot put and the discus throw, a couple more off to the side doing long jumps. Tsali would have the oval track to himself.

"Comrade, greetings!" The words hit Rosie's ears like the stinging pebbles that had been bullets in the water. Comrade! Who the hell had nerve enough to call him that? Rosie turned around and found a tall man, just about his same size and musculature—that is very big, and very muscular—standing there with a hand stuck out. "Greetings to the Third World Enslaved in the United States."

Rosie stared down at the open palm reaching toward him and contemplated the ease with which he could break that hand. He looked back up to the speaker. He was blond and blue-eyed with a round Slavic face.

"You jiving me?" Rosie asked incredulously.

The smile was erased from the big man. "I am Dmitri Blyushkin. I am here to train freedom-fighting members of the Third World for the athletic glory of—"

Rosie turned to the black kid who had suddenly appeared at Blyushkin's side. "Who you?" he demanded.

"Maka Sefa, of Brundasi." The black youth had an angry, defiant look about him. The kind that made Rosie just want to slap him across the face . . . hard.

"Brundasi, huh." Rosie tried to remember which colony had

taken that silly name. Probably meant something like "Fragrant Heaps of Gazelle Shit" in the native language.

The kid had skin as dark as Rosie's. That was very dark. He had the proud flaring nose of a pure African. It didn't look like any oppressing European daddies had cut into his bloodlines. Some kind of daddy should have cut into his fanny, though, that was for sure. Somebody should wipe that snotty expression off him.

"What you running here?" Rosie demanded.

Maka was taken aback. He was used to the ritual that had engulfed the Third World games, the "Comrade this" and the "Comrade that" crap that Rosie wasn't having any time for.

"I will run the ten-thousand meter."

"Oh?" Rosie grinned. Tsali was all set. "Why don't you take a spin with my kid here, a pure-blooded Cherokee Indian. Boy, you have never seen anything as Third World as this one."

Tsali had heard the conversation and was looking over at Rosie speculatively.

"Of course, healthy competition is what the games are provided for," Dmitri announced.

Maka looked over at Tsali and shrugged. "If he would like. I do not think he can compete with me. I will run in the Olympics of 1988. I will win the gold for revolution and for Africa."

Gold, my ass. Rosie smiled in vast self-control. "Fine, we'll just time the two of you." He went over to Tsali and took the kid aside for a moment. "Don't win," he said.

Tsali's eyes opened wide with shock.

"No, no, don't win. It's a kind of psych thing you gotta learn. This boy's so full of himself he thinks he's gonna walk away with this race. You let him think that until the right time. We need time, Tsali, we need lots of time. And I'm gonna talk to this guy who could read the instructions on those tanks we found yesterday."

Tsali obviously wasn't pleased. But he also understood an order when it was given. If he had it in him, he would have tried to be sullen. But there was no point to that if he had a job to do, and losing to Maka Sefa was evidently part of his assignment.

The two teenagers took their mark. Rosie let Dmitri count down and then they were off. The ten-thousand-meter race was a little over six American miles. It would be a little over half an hour before the pair had finished enough laps to make up that distance.

"So, you here to help the poor black folk," Rosie said blandly.

Dmitri Blyushkin nodded with sublime self-confidence. "I train their bodies and I instruct their minds."

The two boys were making their first lap. Tsali was letting Maka have about five strides on him. It must really hurt the kid, Rosie thought.

It hurt Rosie almost as much to watch the African adolescent. There had been a time—Rosie remembered it well—when he had bought into the whole Third World bullshit. The crap had been seductive. It helped him make sense of the senselessness of the ghetto. But no more. There had been lots of reasons for the change in his attitude. He had seen what the "revolution" had done to Newark and Detroit and other cities. That had been a big part. He had learned that the slaves who had been transported to the Western Hemisphere weren't just the victims of white greed. To get there, they had to be caught. Wasn't the English or the Spanish or any of the rest of them that had done the catching, it was other black men. Their *brothers* in Africa.

Then there'd been Vietnam. And he'd seen that black soldiers and black marines and black sailors were just as liable to turn cowards as anyone else, to display greed and show malice.

When you were in Vietnam you just clung to the few good men you were lucky enough to come across. The ones that Rosie had found were a half-breed Cherokee, a quiet Greek, a coked-up blond flyboy, and a crazy-assed idiot who happened to be a shrimpy Jew from New Jersey.

After that, you believe in the United Nations and you do not believe in the superiority of the black race. You believe in good men.

"So, you a Russian?" Rosie finally asked, as he and Blyushkin watched the two boys.

"No, not Russian, Bulgarian." That was almost as weird as coming from somewhere with a stupid-assed name like Brundasi.

Rosie put up with a stream of crap for the next half hour. Blyushkin was as bad as Applebaum, Rosie could swear he was. No, he was worse. How could that be? Well, by the time you've listened to tirades about the noble and self-sacrificing workers of Bulgaria and their solidarity with the benighted revolutionaries of Brundasi, you got to wishing that Marty was there instead, talking about blowing people's heads off.

It was even worse when the facts behind the establishment of Brundasi began to slip back into Rosie's mind. Brundasi, Brundasi . . . Oh, that one. That was the one where a corporal in the army had led a coup. Right, Rosie was letting it all come back now. So this corporal was under a colonel, the ranking member of the armed forces in that little piece of worthless jungle that didn't have room for generals. This colonel made the corporal shine his shoes. Which made the corporal feel like he was a piece of gazelle shit.

So the corporal and two of his friends got the colonel alone in a room, and they shot him. It so happened that the president of the country was with the colonel at the time, so they shot him too, for good measure. Got to the radio and announced a new regime. It so happened that the Brits and the French were occupied elsewhere that day, and by the time anyone had woken up to the facts, the corporal had become the Revered President in Perpetuity. He'd decided that his dictatorship should be called a People's Republic because when you did that, the Russians knocked on your door with a satchel full of gold.

The Revered President in Perpetuity decided that this nation of blacks shouldn't put up with any Asian riff-raff. So they expelled the Indian population that for two hundred years had established trading posts in Brundasi, insuring a favorable balance of trade. That looked good, at least for the time being, so the Revered President went a bit further and kicked out the Europeans as well. Europeans used to be colonials, though not particularly in Brundasi, so they shouldn't stay. That got rid of the businessmen, the doctors, the pilots, most of the teachers, and every administrator capable of drawing up a budget. In less than six months the Revered President in Perpetuity had erased the civilizing effects of two centuries.

Six months later a Brundasi citizen died of starvation—the first time that had happened in over eighty years.

Others died, and the Revered President decided he needed aid, so he turned to the Russians, who were waiting patiently at the door with their satchel of gold. The Revered President set up a bank account in Switzerland, and more people died of starvation. In the meantime, of course, the Russians got a foothold in that part of Africa they hadn't enjoyed before.

Damn, thought Rosie, niggers could be stupid!

The kids were finishing the final lap. They crossed the line and then slowed down, cooling themselves with heads thrown back and with high steps that took them around in quieting circles.

They finally made their way back to Rosie and Blyushkin. Maka slapped Tsali's back. "You did not do badly," he said with condescension that made Rosie grind his teeth. "Someday you will be a good runner. I slowed down so you would not be too far behind me. We are all brothers."

"Until the race, at least," Blyushkin said with a smile.

Rosie watched Tsali carefully. He knew damn well the kid had stayed a regulation distance behind the African runner to fulfill his orders—and he knew damn well that Maka Sefa had worked hard to increase the distance between them but had failed.

Tsali smiled a tight, hard smile—probably the first bitterness he had ever really shown, Rosie thought. Why was it that, at his age, everything had to be a goddamn *lesson?*

Both Maka Sefa and Blyushkin were evidently waiting for Tsali to respond to the African's speech, but Rosie announced, "Kid can't talk. Been mute from birth."

He threw a warmup jacket across Tsali's shoulder and added in a lower tone, "And a damn good thing you can't—right?"

# 17

Rosie had never been so happy to see Marty and Harry before. "My men!" He held out his palms and received a high five from each of them. Marty's was enthusiastic and exaggerated, Harry's quick and almost embarrassed.

Harry and Marty put down their bags and looked around the hotel room. Looked pretty much like the one they had just checked out of in Las Vegas.

Tsali knocked on the door and came into the room with a warm smile of welcome for the new arrivals.

"Tsali, kid, how they hanging?" cried Marty. "You got laid yet? Tsali, I got this carrot crotch out in Vegas, man, she was the sweetest piece of—"

"You bring any rifles? Ammo? Something to fight with?" Rosie's pressing question interrupted the beginning of what would have probably been a substantial detailing of Marty's experiences in Las Vegas. "I mean," said Rosie ruefully, "I brought down this little Austrian Glock-seventeen, one fine pistol: plastic frame, no recoil, nice and simple, but too small for us now; and old Tsali here don't have fuck-all. And man, day before yesterday, we sure could have used something."

"Already?" Harry asked soberly. "That bad?"

"Unbelievable," said Rosie, and told them about the frogmen, the fight in the water, the Cyrillic lettering on the oxygen tanks.

"Look," he concluded, "we were just down here scouting. Not even that. Just setting up our cover, waiting for you guys to show. And then all of a sudden we got dead bodies and we got Russian writing and we got I don't know what all kinds of shit going down. And I got one goddamn little Glock-seventeen. So we got to get ready."

"Shit," said Marty, "we didn't bring anything. We were in Vegas, Rosie. I mean . . ." He trailed off. Applebaum hated being without a gun, but Harry forbade it on vacations. Three Black Berets, four with Tsali, and they had one tiny weapon between them.

"The embassy?" Harry suggested.

"No," said Rosie. "No way." Other times the Berets had pulled on Beeker's lifelong marine umbilical cord to get emergency sidearms from the marine detachment that could be found at every U.S. Embassy. But they'd need more than sidearms this time, and besides, they didn't want *anybody* to know about the presence of an extramilitary force. "Beeker wouldn't want us anywhere *near* that embassy. They're officially ignoring us, Tsali and me being revolutionaries and all, and consorting with Communists."

"Well, we gotta get *something*," protested Marty. "*Somewhere.*"

"We'll call Cowboy." Harry was as easygoing as ever. Told that a bunch of weirdo frogmen had invaded a country, all he said was "I'm hungry. They got room service in this hotel?" Rosie shut his eyes, wondering about the two men who'd just arrived. One crazy as the next.

Harry had already picked up the telephone. He talked to an operator in makeshift Spanish, evidently asking for one who spoke English. He must have gotten his wish. Harry usually did. When a woman heard that voice that seemed a vocal embodiment of all the sadness that suffused Harry's soul, the first thing she wanted to do was help. Any way she could. Any way Harry would let her. In only a couple of minutes, Harry was talking to Cowboy.

"Gotta have some heavy-duty stuff," he said calmly. "You know, like there was war, not just a little bitty thing in the street."

"Don't care how much it costs," Rosie said hurriedly to Harry. "We can afford it. So tell Cowboy to just order it."

"I want bombs, I want grenades, I want Claymores . . ." Marty was making up a little shopping list on a pad of hotel stationery.

"Yeah," said Harry in the telephone. "Soon as possible. Oh, and pick out some toys for Marty."

Harry hung up the telephone, and shrugged as if to say, All right, that's taken care of. He turned to Tsali and said, "How you doing, Tsali? You looking good on the track?"

Tsali was still nursing his bruised ego after the fake practice with the African. The boy shrugged.

"Harry," yelled Rosie, "there is not gonna be any Tsali down on the racetrack next week, and there is not gonna be any of us to watch him if we don't get some goddamn arms!"

Rosie regretted the outburst immediately. Harry and Tsali both looked at him with expressions of hurt.

"Rosie," said Harry, "I did what I could. If there's a major arms supplier in the neighborhood, I'll be glad to go out and pick up a few things. But if there isn't, we're gonna have to wait for Cowboy. And as long as we're waiting for Cowboy, I thought I'd find out how the kid was doing."

"Damn," said Rosie. "Sorry, Harry. I didn't mean—"

"It's all right," said Harry. "Come on, Tsali. Let's go downstairs and I'll buy you a Coke."

The two of them left the room, and Rosie knew that he was getting paid back. They did that on purpose, the assholes. They knew precisely what they were doing, pulling that stuff, going out together and not inviting him. They were leaving him alone with Applebaum, that's what they were doing. If he ever went to hell, Rosie knew what it would be like. A hotel room, with just him and Marty Applebaum inside it. "Rosie, I tell you, this redhead could do things with her . . ."

Rosie closed his eyes. Maybe it was just as well that he didn't have any major weapons at the moment.

# 18

Before Beeker had called the Black Berets back into being, Cowboy had spent years smuggling anything that was worth the trouble of sneaking across a border. Most of it had been dope, and much of that dope his beloved cocaine. But there had been times when the cargo had been so heavy it had affected how high he could fly and how far. He was no fool. The shipments usually were going into countries that would pop up in the headlines in another month or two.

Revolutions and wars did that, got into the headlines. But before they could gather all that media attention they had to have guns loud enough to wake up the American press. Guns made heavy cargoes.

After Harry's call from the hotel room in Huasteca, Cowboy went into action. It had been easy for him to reestablish old contacts. It hadn't been much more than a year since he'd stopped his freelance air ferry service. He called Houston, then Miami, and then made a flying trip to New Orleans. He sat back then, confident that Harry and Rosie and Marty would be taken care of.

Cowboy was taken care of too. He'd scored coke so fresh, it still smelled of the lockers at the Miami airport.

Down in San Sebastian, Harry and Marty followed Cowboy's orders to the letter. It'd been easy enough to buy a four-wheel drive Toyota and hire a guide to lead them, the two men following in their own car, to the abandoned airstrip seventeen miles from Huasteca. The weeds were high, and you couldn't see the asphalt till you were on it. The control tower—a shack on stilts—had fallen into ruin, and the Central American jungle was encroaching on every side. This sneak attack was going to take a few years to implement, but the environment was going to have its own back again.

A bribe larger than his pay in bringing them out convinced the guide that he ought to drive back to Huasteca and forget everything he knew about the two men in the Toyota.

Marty suggested that they blow the man's head off, which would virtually insure his silence, but Harry pointed out that—in general—it wasn't a good idea to kill innocent people. Marty didn't seem terribly disappointed, as if he'd expected his friend to take that position in the matter.

The men that Cowboy dealt with demanded punctuality in payment. In return, they gave punctuality of delivery. When Harry first heard the drone of the twin-prop plane he glanced at his watch. It was only two minutes later than promised. Cowboy would have turned up his nose, but for Harry it was good enough.

Marty had been hiding from the sun inside the truck, looking at the pictures in a Spanish comic book and trying to figure out the story, and he came out and waited beside Harry.

Quickly the plane came into view and swept down for its pinpoint landing. Even a plane so light as this did damage to the runway, cracking apart even more of the deteriorating asphalt surface. Harry and Marty stepped a few feet out of the way, and the plane taxied up close to them.

The door opened, and the pilot peered out. He was wearing sunglasses just like the kind Cowboy always had on.

"I'm the Greek," said Harry.

The pilot nodded, disappeared, and a few moments later, pushed open the cargo door from inside.

"Look," he said, "San Sebastian ain't got the best air defense system in the world, but I'd just as soon get my ass out of here."

"Got it," said Harry.

As the pilot shoved crates over to the bay, and then out over the lip, Harry and Marty lifted them down and placed them in the high grass beside the runway. Harry looked up at the white clouds scudding across the sky, and the brilliant sun, and the surrounding jungle, and he caught Marty's eye across the top of the crate.

"Yeah," said Marty, "I know."

Just like 'Nam.

All in all, nine crates. The heaviest were the ones that contained ammunition. Some with German lettering, some with English, and some with Spanish.

"Spanish?" said Marty, looking at it upside down. "What does it say?"

"CETME. Madrid, Espana," said Harry. "I can't read the rest."

"Fuck," said Applebaum, kicking the crate as soon as they'd put it down. "Cowboy bought us spic guns to fight in a spic country! What kind of shit is this?"

"Cowboy?" said the pilot, looking up at the mention of the name. "This is from Cowboy?"

Neither Harry nor Marty said anything. You didn't exchange information with strangers who were delivering things that nobody ought to know about.

The pilot took their silence for confirmation.

"Oh, shit," he said, for evidently the name Cowboy made a very concrete impression on his mind. "Listen, I really don't want to know what's in those crates. There's one more—" He disappeared for a moment and then quickly pushed the last crate out through the bay—so quickly that it would have crashed to the runway, if Marty and Harry had not rushed up to take it. "And now I'm gonna get the hell out of this place. Good luck to you guys, and don't nobody never tell me how it turned out, okay?"

Harry and Marty had barely got the last crate out of the way when the plane revved up again, turned around in a small circle—but bumpity-bumping as it swerved out through the grass to complete its turn—and then headed off down the runway again. It lifted off at the very end, seemed momentarily in danger of taking off the tops of a few trees, and then suddenly soared away to the northeast.

The two Black Berets were left out in the middle of the deserted airstrip, all alone, with a little over two hundred thousand dollars' worth of munitions—that is, if they hadn't been bilked on the shipment. Harry knew he might have insisted that the cargo be checked before the pilot left, but he was pretty confident of the weight that Cowboy could pull. Nobody messed with Cowboy, not before he became a Black Beret. And certainly not afterward.

Marty was still studying the box with the Spanish label. "Oh, yeah, I can't believe this—that Cowboy would have sent us some kind of shit like this."

"Some kind of shit like what?" said Harry. "You don't even know what's inside, do you?"

Marty looked at his friend. "Gotta be shit. Whoever heard of a Spanish weapon? Those—"

Then he remembered. His eyes lighted up. "Oh, Harry, you think—"

"I do think," said Harry. With his bare hands, he pulled

open the top of the crate. The smell of oil and metal spilled up out of the container. He reached in with one hand and tried to draw out the already assembled weapon, but it was clamped down. Marty leaned in feverishly with a screwdriver that he'd brought in his pocket and quickly made a few turns.

Harry had recognized the machine gun right away. Marty was always dragging him from mercenary show to firearms exhibit, different ones all across the country. The bravado and the bragging and the camouflage clothing for kids had always been too much for Harry. He'd learned that the way to pass time at those things was to attend all the weapons demonstrations. There were always examples of the latest, state-of-the-art arms.

He'd seen this baby once. Just once when it was first introduced into the market. It was the Ameli, a light, highly efficient, highly effective machine gun developed in Spain as an improvement over some German designs. The thing could shoot 1,250 rounds of .223 cartridges a minute. It weighed only fifteen pounds, something of a technological wonder—especially compared to the much heavier M-60 that Marty loved so much.

"Pretty gun, Marty," said Harry.

Marty liked it. Harry could see that. But he didn't want to give up his anger yet. Marty liked to get angry and blow off steam. He'd come back to the Ameli, but because there wasn't anything to object to about it, he started looking in a few of the other crates. "Shit, look at this, Harry, pistols. Cowboy sent us pistols. Pussies use pistols." He kicked at a box of dynamite in his frustration.

Harry knew that the dynamite had to have a detonator to explode, but he still didn't like to see people kicking at boxes of the stuff. Old-fashioned, he guessed.

"Come on, Marty, let's load these things up. Rosie's waiting."

"*Pistols!*"

# 19

Beeker stood at the window of the room on the third floor of the San Sebastian Embassy and looked out at the dusk over Washington. Sunsets in the capital city were often very beautiful, though Delilah had pointed out the reason for this was that D.C. had one of the worst cases of pollution in the country. The poisonous chemicals that rose from one of the highest concentrations of automobiles in the world were the cause of the refracted and reflected glory of the declining sun.

He looked out over the hilly neighborhood and thought that it was a handsome area too: a collection of some grand Federal-style mansions done in a manner worthy of an embassy or a major government agency. But Beeker knew that not very far away—a mile, maybe two miles—Washington was a sewer of tenements, slums worthy of some of the poorest nations of the world, though they seldom had to be viewed by the diplomats and government officials who shuttled back and forth between their racially and economically protected enclaves.

There was a knock at the door, and Beeker turned. He caught a glimpse of himself in the mirror and frowned. He was wearing a black suit, complete with vest, that Delilah had picked out for him at some store called Brooks Brothers that afternoon. Damn, the fabric scratched. At least it didn't bind and cut the way most other suits did. He supposed it must be a good one. God knows they paid enough for it.

"Come," he said.

Delilah walked in. Wearing a low-cut, shimmering blue gown. "Good. You're almost ready."

He suffered her to approach.

"What are you thinking about?" she asked, with her hands at his neck, straightening his tie.

"How soon I can get out of these clothes? How soon I can get out of this building? I hate this business."

"Just stand up straight and think about those two hundred acres, William," said Delilah. "And remember that though you may not like Victorio Salazar very much, he has been a very good president for his people and a very good friend to the United States. Now," she said, stepping back and critically observing her work, "are we ready to go downstairs?"

They made a tour of the rooms on the ground floor. The servants were setting up for the reception that would mark the last evening of President Salazar's visit to the U.S. More than three hundred persons had been invited, including all the members of the Senate Committee on Central American Relations. Two teenage San Sebastian boys in red uniforms were unpacking one of several cases of champagne. Dom Perignon.

"Poverty-stricken Third World?" Beeker asked in quiet sarcasm.

Delilah shrugged. "This is not a waste, you know. If an embassy spends a few thousand dollars on a party like this, entertaining a few members of Congress and the State Department, then they'll get full return on the money. A senator who drinks your Dom Perignon will feel duty-bound to vote you a few million in aid next month. After all, it's not money out of the senator's pocket."

They checked all the ground-floor rooms, just looking around, and then emerged into the small walled garden at the back, riotous with bright spring flowers. The setting sun gilded everything it touched.

It was supposed to be tonight.

They'd figured out most of the note. The man behind the Punch and Judy booth had been the first shot at Salazar. In case he failed—as he had—there was a backup, a different plan entirely, and all that Delilah and Beeker knew about this second plan was that it would be implemented in Washington.

Since Salazar was departing for Huasteca in the morning and would not leave the house till then, the assassination attempt would take place either at this party or tomorrow, on the way to the airport.

It seemed improbable, even to Billy Leaps Beeker, that on a spring evening as lovely as this one, his job was to thwart a murderer. Delilah checked her watch. "It's nearly six. We should go inside. And"—she smiled with a hint of irony—"try to be inconspicuous, will you?"

That was difficult, as it turned out. They returned to the main reception room and stationed themselves in a corner from which they had a view of whoever came through the doors and greeted President Salazar and the ambassador. Delilah stood with a tulip glass of champagne to which she pressed her lips, but never drank. Beeker didn't even have a glass. His way of being inconspicuous was to stand ramrod straight, his arms crossed over his chest, his legs a little apart, his hips thrust slightly forward. He looked like a cigar-store Indian who'd had a suit put on him by the haberdasher next door.

He hated this whole business. The hundreds of guests—very colorful, and lively, chattering in two dozen tongues, and swilling the expensive champagne.

After a quarter of an hour, Delilah left him and took up a position much nearer the president. Sitting on a small chair just behind him, pretending to be entranced by a plate of little sandwiches on her lap and the glass of champagne on the polished floor beside her. But Beeker knew that she was keeping an eye on the president and that should anyone do *anything*, she'd be right there. That smile of hers was on its "hold" button. Beeker hated it. She dazzled everyone who came near her. It looked so real, so inviting. The men, especially, couldn't help but respond to it, and she'd chat with anyone who came near. He knew it was part of her cover, but Beeker hated to watch. He hated it because he was never sure what the difference was between *this* party smile and the one he got in the bedroom alone with her.

He felt the familiar constriction in his underwear, the way it always got when he thought about Delilah in a bedroom. It pissed him off to react so automatically, his hard-on as immediate and unavoidable as her smile at this party. Damn!

"Hello . . ."

With a large smile on her face, the woman in front of him was staring down at his trousers. She was positioned in such a way to screen his source of embarrassment from anyone else in the room—or perhaps to keep it to herself. She took Beeker's nod as an encouragement. "I am Vera Sumarokova," she said. "Of the Bulgarian Embassy."

Beeker blinked. He'd been thinking of a way to get rid of her. But the *Bulgarian* Embassy. The assassin's note had been in a Bulgarian code.

Beeker studied Sumarokova. Her eyes had a slightly oriental

cast to them. Her skin was stark white, like Delilah's, but her hair was deep black. Maybe a little Turkish blood mixed in.

"My name is Beeker," he said.

"Are you South American? Are you Inca?"

"I'm American," said Beeker coldly. "Cherokee."

She thought for a moment, glancing down at his Brooks Brothers trousers again. "Cherokee? They're native to this country, are they not?"

"*We* are," said Beeker, with a slight edge in his voice.

If Sumarokova had been taller, he might have thought that she had recognized him as a bodyguard and was attempting to block his view. But she was not tall—about the same height as Delilah, in fact—and he had no trouble in seeing over her head. Delilah was still on watch behind Salazar.

Vera Sumarokova nodded, as if with a subtle admission of her faux pas. "You are with the State Department."

"No," said Beeker. "I am a guest."

Vera smiled cynically. "Yes, yes, I understand. It is very fashionable to invite Native Americans these days—and the idea of a Third World nation within the United States appeals to the country's sense of justice. I—*of course*—think that this is a good thing. We are always anxious to have the oppressed peoples of the world represented in order to show our . . . *solidarity*."

There was no question what she meant when she said *solidarity*. The word was aimed right at his crotch.

Billy Leaps caught Delilah's eye at that moment. A very slight indication of her head told them it was time to make a circuit of the party, as they'd agreed upon beforehand.

"Another time," said Beeker to Vera Sumarokova, and slipped away.

But as he did so, he looked at Delilah and then very slightly cast his eye back to Vera, as if to say: Keep an eye on this one . . .

Delilah inclined her head a fraction of an inch, but that told Beeker she understood.

The rooms were crowded, and Beeker edged his way through, not looking for anything in particular, but just keeping his eyes open. Letting the impressions come as they would. It was the only way to see something that was out of kilter, to take in everything and let the normal and the safe sift through.

When you're looking for a well-executed plan to take effect, you have to expect it to strike from the least expected place. The most usual and obvious invasion routes the enemy could have taken had been covered. The servants had all been checked out; they had gone through metal detectors earlier in the day and had been refused permission to leave the embassy afterward. Beeker himself had gone through all their supplies. Sure, one of them could take a fruit knife and hurl himself at Salazar, but Delilah was sitting with her little plate of sandwiches and her tulip glass of champagne in order to prevent something like that.

They were dealing with a sophisticated attacker. The attempt near the Capitol had been top-notch. It was actually only a lucky break that Beeker had spotted the assassin when he did. The glint of the reflection on the gun barrel couldn't have been foreseen. Of course, the assassins couldn't have predicted that the leader of the Black Berets was going to be walking around the area at that time either. Too bad.

But what would it be now?

The ladies all had their little bags, plenty large enough for a deadly pistol. The men had their suits, and a pistol could be concealed beneath a looseness of fabric, or in a pocket beneath a set of long coat tails, or behind the plastering of medals on the chest. There might even be a bomb somewhere, which would kill Salazar effectively enough but would probably take out a few bystanders as well.

Salazar himself had taken no special precautions. He'd been shot at before, had bombs planted beneath the hood of his car, knives stuck through his thigh, hypodermics full of poison pricked into his skin. He'd survived all those interesting incidents, and intended to survive this one.

Beeker found nothing out of order in the reception rooms, and noticed only that Vera Sumarokova was following him about in a vague but possibly meaningful manner. She was Bulgarian, the assassin was Bulgarian, but it wasn't entirely certain that she knew about the attempt. For all he knew, she might be a secretary. And when the bomb went off, and the blame was laid at the Bulgarian door, they would say, "But one of our own people died!"

The colorful lanterns had just been lighted in the garden, though there was still a low layer of pink and gold clouds in the west. The bartender clinked glasses and ice together as he mixed drinks, and the conversation out there was low and murmuring. The ten-foot walls protected the guests from the breeze that was blowing in off the Potomac . . .

*The walls!*

# 20

Beeker stiffened. He had to appear calm. He lifted one foot and rested it on the stone seat at the edge of the patio. He leaned one elbow on his knee and scanned the crowd of people gathered. They were chatting comfortably in that way he despised about cocktail parties. One of them, or perhaps two, would know. He just had to figure out which ones.

That the attack would come over the wall directly behind him he no longer had any doubt. If was a feeling, but one of the most valuable lessons he'd learned in life was to trust his instinct, and not to say, That doesn't figure . . .

It was a couple who were waiting. A man and a woman. He saw them in the opposite corner of the garden. Their smiles were artificial and unchanging. They weren't even talking with one another, but it was obvious they were discouraging anyone else from approaching them. It was the quick and practiced glances toward the wall behind him that gave them away to Beeker. That, and how frequently the man checked his watch—without actually moving his wrist.

It would be easy. Just so very easy. Maybe he should just take them out.

El Presidente wouldn't like that though. Damn politicians have to have proof every time. They didn't go on their own instincts, and they certainly wouldn't go on Beeker's. They can't take a soldier's word for it. If Billy Leaps had just done what should be done, he knew he wouldn't be able to provide hard evidence that the dead man and the dead woman had been plotting to kill Salazar.

So he couldn't do it.

The result? Salazar's life was in greater danger. So was Beeker's, and so was Delilah's, and so was the life of anyone who stood between this wall and President Salazar in the front reception room. Say about two hundred seventy-five innocent, well-dressed people. Because Beeker would have to wait for a move to be made.

Beeker waited. He studied a young woman who was standing close to the couple, close enough that his stares in her direction gave him a perfect peripheral view of the man and woman he was convinced were the source of the real danger.

He would wait it out, get his proof, take them . . .

"I prefer the evening air as well," Vera Sumarokova said.

"Yeah," said Beeker, giving her only the quickest, and not the friendliest, glance.

He still couldn't tell if she was in on it. Logic told him she was, but instinct hesitated. There was a motive behind what she did, and it wasn't purely lust, but if it wasn't lust, and it wasn't the death of Salazar, then what—

"You find that young woman beautiful?" Her question had the air of scientific examination about it.

Beeker seemed to see the young woman across the garden for the first time, really, though he'd been watching her for several minutes. "Yeah, I do," he said. She'd stood out because of her height, probably five eleven. Slender, though sleek might be a better word. There was good tone to the muscles of her bare upper arms. "She an athlete?" Beeker asked.

"She is Nadia Ozerova, one of Bulgaria's finest tennis players."

So, even when he was looking at someone besides his target, he was getting a focus on another one of them. "Lots of Bulgarians at a Central American party," he remarked, then wished he hadn't. Because he should have noticed only two: Vera Sumarokova and the tennis player. The man and woman who were waiting for someone to slip over the wall shouldn't have come into his ken.

But Vera didn't pick up on the mistake. "We could eliminate one of them from this gathering very quickly, very effectively," she said.

Billy Leaps frowned, not understanding what she meant by that.

"Take me home," she explained. "It will mean one less Bulgarian here."

"No. Came with someone."

"Leave with someone else."

He shook his head no.

"A shame." Vera put a hand on Beeker's upper arm and squeezed slightly. At first it seemed an affectionate gesture, then he realized she was testing the goods. She liked what was underneath the fabric. "A very great shame." Her eyes took him in, wandering over his suit-clad torso. Jesus Christ, she was looking at him as if he were some piece of meat hanging in a butcher's locker.

Beeker put his foot back down on the ground, off the stone seat. His arms assumed their protective posture over his chest. "Sorry, it's all spoken for."

She shrugged. "I must leave in any event." She looked at her watch. "I was simply hoping for some . . . distraction."

Vera turned her back and walked away from Beeker. It seemed that she was purposely moving her body in a seductive way, expecting him to be studying her ass.

That lady's dangerous, he thought. When he looked away from her and back to Nadia Ozerova, he got a quick insight into just how dangerous. Ozerova was scowling at him with obvious hatred and disgust. All the pieces fell into place at once. Vera certainly was playing a dangerous game. She was using Beeker to make her girlfriend jealous. Jesus Christ.

Ozerova stalked into the house a few moments later. Now he knew that Sumarokova and Ozerova were not part of the plot at all, and he was glad of that. Two fewer to have to worry about.

But now he had nothing to direct his attention to as he watched the couple. He went over to the white-clothed table and ordered a Scotch from the bartender. "Lots of ice," he said, but that didn't matter because he wasn't going to drink it anyway. He returned to his place and sat down on the stone bench, turned in the direction of the couple by the wall. If he hadn't been studying them so intently before, he wouldn't have recognized that the man and woman were distinctly more agitated.

The change was subtle. But the glances toward the wall were more frequent, and undisguised. So was the checking of the time.

Beeker was moving into peak. He could feel the adrenaline flowing through his body, the tension beginning to tighten his muscles. His eyes were hardened, he knew that as well. The concentration he applied was total. This was it.

It happened quickly. Just the way Beeker figured it would. There was the sound of rubber soles scraping on stone above and behind him. A quick scream from one of the guests near him. Sudden moves by the couple he'd been surveying. Then as he finally turned, two figures jumped down from the top of the wall onto the patio.

They wore ski masks that covered all their heads, leaving slits only for eyes and mouth. Each man carried two automatic rifles, AK-47s, and with one practiced motion the two intruders threw the rifles in their right hands into the air.

The man and the woman caught them.

The four of them were obviously going to blast their way through the patio door and toward Salazar. This would be an assassination as loud and ugly as the first attempt had been quiet and understated.

But before any of the murderous quartet had gotten off a round, Beeker was behind the two masked men.

They were not prepared for him. Their concentration was clearly focused on the path they'd have to take toward the house. Beeker had moved quickly and silently right up to them. He spread his arms wide and caught the two men's heads on the outside. Then he slammed their heads together, hard. It was like pounding two unripe canteloupes together, except canteloupes don't have bones inside, and they don't moan when they crack open, and blood doesn't gush out of them when they bounce off stone walls.

The noise alerted the other two. They were in the doorway, and attempted to swing round. But there wasn't room for the AK-47s to make the turn, and there was a bit of fumbling. By the time they had the rifles in position, Beeker was there.

The male was easy. Beeker just took his two palms and used the favorite marine attack. He slammed each hand over one of the man's ears. The sudden force and change in pressure inside the head ruptured his eardrums, producing excrutiating pain, the likes of which this guy had never felt, the kind of pain where you can't hold things in your hands and you have to drop them.

The AK-47 clanked on the flagstone patio. As it bounced, Beeker had moved against the woman. She looked strange in a full-length gown, her long hair up and dressed with flowers, holding the automatic rifle and raising it against Billy Leaps. But she wasn't quick enough. A roundhouse punch shattered her nose, and a flood of blood and mucus spilling down her throat strangled even her scream.

Now would come the part Beeker hated the most about these scenes—the screams, the pandemonium of the bystanders who'd so rarely, or never, seen death in this brutal form.

But there was no scream, just a shuffling of feet as guests and servants backed away.

After all, these were diplomats, and diplomats—like miners, and deep-sea divers, and racing-car drivers—knew that they'd taken up a dangerous profession. Sudden death was unpleasant, but it wasn't totally unexpected.

There was no pandemonium, but the guests on the patio reentered the house by a side door, while the guests in the room just inside the house slowly backed into a room where there weren't any corpses.

Only Delilah fought the tide of retreating guests. She came into the room and glanced at the two bodies lying in the open doorway. The man was still alive, though unconscious. The woman was still, and might be dead. Beeker had collected their rifles.

"Two more out here," said Beeker. "They're dead."

Delilah nodded. "May I pour you a drink?"

# 21

Rosie Boone was not the kind of man who should be riding a bicycle. But he was. All six-foot-two and two hundred twenty pounds of him were pedaling through the streets of Huasteca. Ahead of him ran Tsali. To any observerer they were simply another athlete-coach team practicing for the Third World games.

No one would doubt that they were Third World. Not with Rosie's coal-black skin glossy with perspiration, or Tsali's square-cut features, brown skin, and glossy black hair worn long in the Cherokee style.

It was a good cover. It was a great cover. This little run through the city was actually one of the soldier's most important tools. Under cover, they were reconnoitering their future battleground. Rosie no longer doubted that it would be just that. Not after eight men in frog suits rose up out of the Gulf of Mexico and two assassination attempts in D.C.

The kid kept up a good pace. It was enough to move them quickly through the city, but not so fast that Rosie couldn't find time to study the various neighborhoods.

He just knew there wasn't a goddamn thing there. Not a

thing going on that could give him a due. The people were happy, and as they passed, they got smiles and sometimes even cheers. He didn't see the gloomy, glowering masses he'd seen in other countries that were about to tip over into revolution. The streets were clean, people had pride in their homes. All of it spelled stability, not revolution.

Tsali was headed back for the hotel now. Damn, what was going on there? Rosie only hoped that the others had had more success. Anything. There had to be some information.

"Nothing," Harry said when the sweaty and panting pair finally stopped before the hotel. The big Greek and the skinny runt Applebaum were sitting at the hotel patio, next to one another at a table, with Harry in the sun and Applebaum cowering in the shade of a large umbrella.

"I left my carrot crotch for this!" Marty said in disgust. "I tell you, even the lousy cops here smile at you. They got nothing, a couple of ancient Colt forty-five revolvers and that's the best armaments we saw in the entire place. Good thing too," Applebaum said with a pout, "since we just got spic guns."

Harry and Rosie didn't even bother to contradict him. They both knew that when the time came, Applebaum would be the first to reach for the Spanish Ameli.

"We're fine from everything I can see," Rosie repeated. "Can't find the trouble center—and there's got to be a center."

"It's the games," said Harry.

"Yeah," Rosie agreed. But you can't have a revolution with just foreigners. He knew that. You had to have locals. "The games, or it's gonna be people in the out-country. People we just haven't seen yet. Tsali, we have to run again tomorrow. Way out, in the sticks."

Tsali's face showed resignation for a moment. Then that disappeared, as if he did not even want to show himself complaining. He wasn't going to argue. But he'd already run more than thirty miles that day, much too much for someone out for the half-marathon. It would have been too much for anyone participating in these games. The sham training was ruining him. He was doing his duty and watching his chances for the gold erode with every one of these observation runs. After these bouts, there wasn't time for his body to rejuvenate itself.

*Now I'll shower and rest,* he signed, and went heavily inside the hotel.

The men out on the hotel patio didn't need to read Tsali's thoughts to understand the cause of his dejection.

"Kid should be able to play kid games," Harry said. No one argued with him.

Rosie followed Tsali in a couple of minutes. When he got to the room he discovered the kid face down on the bed, already asleep. He hadn't even made it to the shower. Rosie went to his trainer's kit and got out the salves he'd brought. He took off Tsali's running shoes and socks and grimaced at what he found.

Tsali had run his feet too often, far too often. No matter how well they'd been conditioned in Louisiana, they couldn't take much more of this punishment. When Rosie applied the salve to his hands and then began to massage one of Tsali's feet, the kid groaned in his sleep from the touch. Rosie could only hope that the salve would help. He spent a long hour rubbing and coaxing the calloused and blistered skin.

In the morning Rosie was damning himself as he and Tsali set out on their mission. The older Black Berets had studied the maps of the countryside and had decided that the northwest sector looked most promising—if only because they'd heard that what poverty there was in San Sebastian was there. The seacoast, to the southeast, was doing well with a flourishing fishing and tourist industry. To the west were large, efficient cattle ranches. The north was coffee-growing country. Maybe on the large plantations there they'd find the festering sore oozing the pus and stink of violence.

There had been some fine handguns in the cache of arms that Cowboy had sent down. Spanish machine guns were only part of the shipment. The SIG/Sauer .38 supers were works of art. The autoloading pistols had been designed by the Swiss and manufactured by the Germans—an unbeatable combination.

Rosie had strapped one of them into a holster. He carried plenty of extra cartridges just in case.

Tsali evidently wanted his own security. He was dressed in his usual running shorts and T-shirt. Around his waist was a leather belt he'd made himself back in Louisiana. Lying along the length of the belt were two long, narrow-bladed knives—two not only for the extra security, but to balance the distribution of extra weight as he ran.

Kid thinks a knife's going to save him in a battle? Rosie thought. Then he remembered some occasions in Vietnam when a knife had come in awfully handy. The grin disappeared from his face.

They put Rosie's bicycle on the back of the Toyota, then set out. The terrain of San Sebastian rose dramatically as they drove northwest from the capital. The hills quickly increased in size and the angle of ascent. The air grew perceptibly cooler. The vegetation was still lush, but it no longer looked like jungle—more like a North American deciduous forest, one not affected by acid rain.

At a village with only a small general store and a gas station, Rosie parked the Toyota. He spoke to the owner of the station in pidgin Spanish and explained that he was going to leave the vehicle there for a while. Then he took off the bike and Tsali followed him out into the road.

"Map says we got to go that direction, Tsali." He pointed toward a steep incline. Tsali closed his eyes. The running would be excruciating there, even worse than it had been down in the valleys of the region around the capital. He nodded yes.

Rosie climbed on the bike and led the way. He let Tsali take the lead as soon as the boy had begun his pace, wanting to be able to see him at all times. The Black Berets knew that the kid's inability to speak meant they had to take special precautions to prevent his muteness from increasing risks.

The big black man pedaled the bicycle along. He watched the form of the youngster in front of him. Tsali seemed to be playing some game of his own. He was pulling out all the stops on this Cherokee pride thing. Rosie figured that must be what was going on.

Tsali was putting on a true class act. Maybe Rosie was the only one who would ever see it, but the black man knew it was there. Tsali was maintaining a perfect pace. His muscles must have screamed. His feet were probably bleeding. His lungs had to be burning with the exertion of pulling in enough oxygen to keep the monster engine of his body going. But the kid was doing it and he was doing it with style.

*I can trust him.* That was the one thing that a warrior could say to another man and, with those words, bestow the greatest possible benediction. I can trust him in battle. I can trust him in my home. I can trust him to pull his weight. I can trust him . . . . Boy's only seventeen, Rosie thought, and he's already one of the best.

# 22

The carefully laid-out rows of coffee bushes marked the edge of the famous San Sebastian coffee region. Coffee comes in many different types. There's the bulk stuff that can be harvested easily with enormous machines, in places like Brazil and Colombia. There's the specialty beans, grown from carefully nurtured trees to preserve the unique flavor imparted by a particular kind of soil. Just like wine—there was Mondavi, putting out millions and millions of cases a year from grapes grown a hundred miles apart, and there were some of the French wineries, putting out a few hundred cases a year, from grapes that were grown on half an acre of land.

San Sebastian coffee was of the latter sort—premium coffee of a dense flavor. The product of these small and intensely cultivated coffee plantations was reserved for those countries who truly appreciate, and can afford to pay for, fine coffee.

It looked to Rosie as if profits might be good. While Tsali maintained his grueling pace, Rosie couldn't see much that was wrong with this northwest region of San Sebastian. The farms were clean and well kept, just like the places they'd passed in the flatlands below. As yet they hadn't come across the poverty that was the breeding ground of revolution.

They had to keep on going. They couldn't give up. It was the soldier who didn't continue to look who later walked into an ambush. Rosie felt terrible about Tsali. But it couldn't be helped. They had to find out what was going on in this country.

There were more coffee plantations to the west. They must have passed some change in the type of soil, Rosie realized, or emerged from the leeward side of some distant mountain. They were still high up, and the ascent still steep. but suddenly they were back into wild country. Once again they were in jungle.

Rosie recalled the map and knew that they were entering the area of San Sebastian that was not totally settled. This was the local equivalent of the old Indian Territory, the place into which the original inhabitants of the country had been forced in the course of centuries of settlement.

Probably some of them Tsali's relatives, Rosie thought. There was something about the area that made Rosie feel the potential danger to them had increased dramatically. He knew that at least part of that sensation was from the fact that the region reminded him of the highlands of Indochina, of Vietnam and Laos, where the mountainous terrain made it so easy for the enemy to hide himself.

If I wanted a staging area for my revolution, this would be it. If I were—

"Tsali! Stop!"

The boy froze. Rosie had braked his bicycle. His warning had been instinctive, and he'd had no idea why he'd called. He put the bike down on the side of the road and covered it with brush, leaving only a little of the handlebar uncovered so that he'd be able to find it again himself.

Tsali had immediately responded to the tone of Rosie's

command. The kid fought with his lungs to get the oxygen back into his system.

When Tsali had recovered himself a little, the two of them moved stealthily up the side of the road. They hadn't yet seen anything, but they acted as if the enemy were behind every tree. And there were a lot of trees.

Rosie drew his German pistol. Tsali had one of his knives out. If there was someone there and if that someone meant them harm, they'd be ready to respond.

Half a mile farther on, they discovered that Rosie's infallible instinct had come through for them.

Was it a random noise of metal and machinery that had reached his ear from such a distance? The accumulation of too many human voices at once, in a brief coincidental chorus that had alerted him? Had too many men made the same step at the same time and sent out a vibration through the ground that Rosie had picked up? Rosie didn't know, but whatever it was had spelled danger to the black man despite its acting at some level that was below his sensory consciousness.

But something had happened. The warning had come somehow, and Rosie knew he'd never be able to explain it. He'd just known that there was danger ahead and he had acted on that certainty. It was the infinite advantage of the trained warrior that he could do that. The pink-skinned grunt fresh from Lejeune never did. Nor did the punk wise-ass on the streets of Harlem. But the older men who had already survived a hundred fights, they knew, they always knew, and that was a big part of how they lasted to fight number one hundred one.

Tsali and Rosie peered carefully into the large and unexpected clearing in front of them. At least three hundred uniformed men were gathered there. Most of them looked like they might be natives of San Sebastian, but Rosie saw uniformed officers that were blond and blue-eyed. Off to a corner were four armored vehicles. Rosie recognized them as Russian T-62s. Again, that was almost an instinctual knowledge. He knew he'd never seen them in action, and he couldn't remember when or where he'd read up on them, but the instant he saw the silhouette, "T-62" came into his mind.

Big mothers with 115-mm guns on the turrets, along with a 7.62-mm machine gun.

No use in a jungle though. Rosie understood that immediately. The bastards—whoever they were—were going to go right down the same road he and the kid drove, and they were going to ride those monsters right into the city of Huasteca.

All those smiles on the citizens' faces were going to get wiped right off.

Made Rosie mad.

He turned to nudge Tsali. They had to get back to tell the others what they'd discovered.

The kid wasn't there.

Tsali's silence was incredible. That Rosie could have discerned the existence of this armed camp and then not register the kid's moving away from him was proof of Tsali's Cherokee stealth.

But this time it made Rosie mad. Well, at least worried. Where had he gone? Still holding his SIG/Sauer .38—though knowing that the most he could use it for was a bludgeon—Rosie inched his way back toward the road. He sure hoped to God he didn't run into any sentries, because there was no way that he and one pistol were going to fight off three hundred men and then take on four Russian tanks.

Suddenly he felt a dart of pain against his forehead.

Someone had thrown a pebble at him.

He turned in the direction it came from, ducking at the same time.

The gun was cocked, though he knew that only under the direst circumstances could he risk firing and drawing the attention of the armed revolutionaries not a hundred yards away.

There was Tsali, holding a finger to his lips. Rosie moved toward the boy. Tsali moved aside, and Rosie saw two corpses on the ground.

Men uniformed like those in the clearing.

One of them had pissed his pants, and Rosie got the stink of that.

When he got closer he saw that each of the men was wearing a red necklace. A semicircle of thick red blood and death.

Flies were already gathering and setting up a buzz that made it seem as though the dead men were trying to whisper reproach at the seventeen-year-old boy who had killed them.

# 23

Intelligence.

Without it you can have the biggest and best army and it wouldn't be worth a damn. With it you can take a guerrilla force and destroy the collective might of a great power. If you know the enemy's secrets, the enormous advantage of his bulk is worthless.

Beeker was gathering intelligence too.

Gathering it in an unlikely place—at Delilah's house in the Virginia countryside. A hundred acres of hilly, forested, and streamed land surrounded them. It was very expensive land. This was the playground of America's super-rich, the rich so rich they could keep their lives secret. This was the country where they rode their horses on make-believe hunts and kept their centuries-old mansions far from the public view.

There were no servants at Delilah's house. Her home was small compared to her neighbors', though it would have been considered a small mansion back in Shreveport. If he'd had the time Beeker would have wondered about that. He couldn't quite imagine Delilah with her hair pinned up, vacuuming the floor or polishing the silver. There must be people to come in and clean up every once in a while. It was just that they were never around when Beeker paid one of his infrequent visits. They were going to have a certain amount of work after this trip.

Beeker was staring down at a man's body that was spread-eagled on a bed in one of Delilah's guest rooms. This was the only one of the four attackers who was in any shape to tell them what they needed to know. Two others were dead. The third was in a D.C. hospital, unconscious and likely to remain so for some time to come. Until they pulled the plug.

The man was naked. He looked ridiculous, though that wasn't his fault. He looked ridiculous because his strongly muscled body was tied to a sturdy colonial bed, complete with embroidered canopy. Delilah obviously hadn't decorated her house with torture sessions in mind. Beeker couldn't help noticing, however, that the bed frame had been reinforced at several points—and there was no way that this guy was going to pull himself free.

Beeker looked over at her. She had a glass of Scotch in her hand. He knew she usually settled for white wine. She must not like this too much, he thought. Well, neither did he. She nodded to Beeker, ready for the interrogation to begin.

Beeker turned to his captive. He wished that Rosie was around. Rosie was good at this sort of thing. Rosie found parts of a man's body he didn't even know he had, and he made those places *hurt*.

There is an etiquette to all things, even torture sessions.

Very politely, before anything began, Delilah asked the man to tell them what they wanted to know.

She spoke in Russian.

The man didn't reply.

She asked the same thing in Bulgarian.

The man's head jerked up in surprise at the sound of his

own language. That surprise told them one thing they'd wanted to know—the man's nationality.

He still didn't tell them anything. And after that, he wouldn't even look at Delilah. Afraid to betray himself again.

It must be strange, Beeker thought, to be lying there with your dork hanging out and your balls on display with a lady in formal gown sipping a drink in the corner. The guy must have been embarrassed. Should have been too, with the size of that shriveled little pecker.

Beeker had been down in Delilah's cellar and picked out a few interesting items at a corner that was given over to woodworking tools. He'd decided he wanted to start the way Rosie did, real subtle.

He had a small brush of stiff wire that was used to scrape paint.

Beeker hefted the strangely soft skin of the man's scrotum. Just enough to let the man know where the first attack was coming. A man didn't like things to happen down there.

The man's mouth opened, as if in preparation for the first groan.

As Beeker, somewhat reluctantly, began his dirty work, Delilah told herself that this was necessary, that thousands of lives depended on this man's information. A fleeting wave of nausea went through her, but she fought it back. This must be done, she kept thinking, as the Bulgarian screamed.

Still, the man didn't talk. Fool, Beeker thought. A man should know that when he's in a torturer's den there's no escape. He might just as well give in at the beginning and hope they'll either off him quickly and without pain, or else that, for whatever reason, the torturers will keep him alive. And if he's kept alive, then there's a possibility of rescue. The one thing certain is that there is no possibility of holding back the requested information—not ultimately. That was what Beeker always told the Black Berets. Don't put yourselves through that agony. Give in. But he knew that none of them ever would. They'd all end up playing hero like this one.

Delilah repeated her questions. Her voice wasn't harsh, she didn't yell. Her tone suggested that they might be there all day, and that must have been a pretty ominous thought for the captive.

He still didn't answer. Damn fool, Beeker thought, as he bent down again to his work.

The Bulgarian screamed again, then shook, gulping and gasping for air.

Beeker took a needle, out of a sewing kit. A long needle.

He held it up for the captive to see.

The Bulgarian stared, and there was terror in his eyes.

Beeker threateningly brought the needle near the man's private parts.

The man began to scream the right answers in Bulgarian.

# 24

"Well?" Beeker was impatient. Delilah had just left him alone for an hour in the living room, while she played in the next room with a computer terminal. On one side of him he'd listened to the whir of the machine and the occasional ring of the telephone, and on the other side of him he'd listened to the two women who'd arrived to take charge of the Bulgarian.

It was past midnight, and he was tired.

He'd sat with a Scotch, and eventually, when the noise from the bedroom left off, he'd got up to look in. The prisoner wasn't there, the two women were gone as well, and the bed was remade. He couldn't even smell the blood that had been spilled there.

In its own way, this was probably a household as peculiar as his own.

But eventually Delilah did come back in, poured a glass of white wine for herself, and took a tray of small sandwiches out of the refrigerator. Definitely not William Leaps Beeker's idea of food and drink—so he refused it.

"Well?" he repeated. "What did we find out?"

She toyed with her glass.

"It's unfortunate," she began, "about what's happened to international sports."

Not how he'd expected her to start out, but at least she'd started. He said nothing.

"They've become totally politicized," she went on. "Carter used them over Afghanistan in eighty. The Russians retaliated in eighty-four. But those are the simplest and most obvious political uses.

"There's a more subtle way they're used—a country can be legitimized through its sports. Red China and Ping-Pong matches shows you just about how silly, and how effective, this sort of thing can be. For Communist countries particularly. Communists, for all their rhetoric about eventual world domination, have a great and abiding need to be seen as normal and upright members of the world community. They can cultivate that image through sports. They send out their strongest and handsomest and most talented, and everybody falls in love with the young athletes, and the world begins to think, 'Well, how bad can the totalitarian regime of Bulgaria be if they've got seventeen-year-olds who smile like that?"

Beeker still didn't understand where she was going with this, and she wasn't telling him anything new yet.

"There's a third way the Communists use these games," she said.

"What?"

"We've never actually seen it in operation, but we've suspected it. We now think that we're going to see it in San Sebastian. I think the Russians are setting this up as a kind of dry run for even more elaborate schemes . . .."

Beeker wanted to say, Just spit it out. But he knew she'd get round to it. With a glass of white wine in her hand, and no naked men bleeding on her bed, Delilah liked to take her time.

"Sports—any kind of cultural exchange, for that matter—gives someone like the Bulgarians a legitimate excuse to be in a country when they know there's going to be a revolution. The coaches, the members of the team, the support staff, even the reporters assigned to the teams will—on a given signal—turn into something else. Pilots, radio technicians, demolition experts, even plain old basic soldiers. The rebels blow the whistle for the start of the revolution, and suddenly, right there, they've got a kind of technological backup force already in place.

"And when it's over—and the Communist rebels are in power—the Bulgarians will simply claim to have been bystanders. To have been unluckily caught between two warring factions. No one will be able to prove otherwise. Ever."

Beeker looked down into his glass. *Tsali.* "Then this thing is bigger than a presidential assassination?"

"The Russians don't care about San Sebastian. But they do care whether their plan will work, and San Sebastian makes a nice little spot for a few war games. Too bad for San Sebastian, of course. And if it succeeds, the Russians will have more than a toehold in Central America. If it fails, it's back to the drawing board for a couple of years, and some stupid general gets demoted, and the general's son is expelled from the University of Moscow."

"In the meantime," said Beeker, "lots of people die."

Delilah nodded.

"Everything is ready in San Sebastian," she said. "They've been bringing in people from all over Central America and setting them up in the hills northwest of Huasteca. They look enough like the natives that they'll pass. And then there are a few natives who actually have sold out. The Russians are looking forward to a very sweet, very easy, very profitable coup. And you'll notice—when we get down there—there's not an actual Russian in sight. They're all Bulgarians."

"Has anybody told the president about this?"

"The president of what country? San Sebastian or the United States?"

"Either one."

"We'll tell Salazar tomorrow," said Delilah. "He of course has the right to know. Our President knows as well. But what can he do? He can't commit troops before a shot is fired; he'd look like an incredible aggressor, and the Russians would make hay out of that. On the other hand, if he waits till the first shot *is* fired, it may be too late. And that is why"—she paused and sipped her wine—"that is why this thing is falling on my head. And on yours, of course."

In the same tone of voice, wives told husbands that they'd just charged too much on the Bloomingdale's card. *You'll just have to pay for it, honey . . ..*

"Do we get any sort of assistance?"

"All the information I have, of course. And I'm arranging for you to have the use of one hell of a copter."

"So," said Beeker, "five guys, one teenage boy, and one hell of a helicopter. And you want us to stop a revolution?"

"Well," she said, "you have until Tuesday . . . ."

# 25

Cowboy had it all figured out. If he got the security system in place, ready for a week's absence, he'd have exactly five minutes to get himself and his Corvette off the property before the sirens went off—and before the road to the house blew up very high into the sky with whatever was unlucky enough to be on it at the time. He could stop safely just beyond the gate and coke up. That would get him to Shreveport. At the airport, he'd get his ticket, and then re-coke in the men's room. That would get him onto the plane. He could coke up there, just before the plane landed in New Orleans. Again in the men's room there, for the two-hour stopover before the flight for San Sebastian took off.

Then all he had to do was be sure he finished off everything he had on that international flight. Just in case the guards searched him in Huasteca, he didn't want to have arms in his suitcase and a vial of cocaine on his body. Didn't make a good impression in Central America, that sort of thing.

Cowboy didn't have much doubt about his ability to finish off whatever he had left on the flight from New Orleans south.

He figured that while he was in New Orleans, he'd call up a

florist and send Sambo's sister a dozen red roses. Sambo's sister sold solid stuff.

Delilah and Beeker sat alone in a small kitchen in a small house in the Cuban section of Miami, gobbling food much better than what they'd been served on the flight down from Washington. It may have burned the lining of their stomachs, but it was real. In the next room, Victorio Salazar was giving a speech to a number of former citizens of San Sebastian, congratulating them on whatever prosperity they'd found in the United States, gently chiding them for leaving a homeland that was the most stable in Central America and looked soon to be the most prosperous, and concluding that they ought all to follow the progress of the Third World games, to begin the following Tuesday, which would bring their beloved San Sebastian in the limelight of the world's stage.

Beeker understood a little Spanish, and Delilah translated parts of the speech that was unclear to him.

It was strange to Beeker—he found that he liked these people, even the ones who had abandoned San Sebastian. He liked kitchens like this, and he liked the notion of thirty people gathering in somebody's living room to hear a national leader give a little speech. It wouldn't have been so terrible to be a part of a life like this. "You know," he said, "I hope that we can help this man."

Tsali and Rosie were sitting at the back of a classroom, each wearing a pair of earphones. They were watching a film entitled *Dealing with the First World*. It had been prepared by the Second World, for the benefit of the Third World, and the narration was in a dozen different languages. Rosie had turned down the sound till it was no more than a low vibration in his ears, and he fell asleep, though he remained stock still with his head turned exactly toward the screen. Tsali watched the film carefully, to see what he could learn about the nations and the peoples discussed. There was no telling where the Black Berets might end up next.

Harry and Marty were driving the Toyota truck back up the same road that Tsali and Marty had traveled earlier.

They were wearing skirts, and Marty didn't like it one little bit.

"This is an insult," he declared. "To me. It is an insult to my *mother*."

"Shut up, Marty. We decided."

Harry seldom made such a direct remark as "Shut up" to anyone, not even to his friend, but he was driving, and he'd been driving a long while, and he was weary of Applebaum's unceasing outrage. Even though he understood it. The problem was, deep inside, in a way he'd never show it, Harry thought it was the funniest thing he'd ever seen.

Martin Applebaum, of the state of New Jersey, was wearing the cassock of a Roman Catholic priest. It didn't suit him. The long skirt seemed to flare out around his spindly bare legs like a bell. The collar scratched his neck and had left a long line of red all round it. The material was stiff and it irritated his skin. Besides that, Applebaum had discovered that there was some plant flowering in San Sebastian that had taken a direct bead on his asthma. He wept continually.

Harry also wore a cassock, but on him it looked more natural. It wasn't surprising to find a priest who was as sad-eyed and serious as Harry. It wasn't surprising to find a priest who was as big as Harry. He might have been a pro-football player who'd undergone a crisis of faith. Nobody would have been tempted to laugh at Harry's skirts.

"I'm Jewish, Harry. Jewish! Jews aren't priests. Why couldn't I have been a rabbi? That would have made sense. I know how rabbis act. I don't know shit about Catholics. My mama used to warn me about Catholics. She said they stole little Jewish boys and would whip them till they bowed down in front of statues and kissed their feet. When I was bad, my mama used to say, 'The Cat-Licks are gonna come and take you away, Martin Applebaum.'"

"Marty, San Sebastian is Catholic, so priests don't stand out. There probably aren't twenty-five Jews in the whole country, so a rabbi would look sort of strange. Lots and lots of priests around here deliver stuff to the people in isolated areas. So if we get stopped they just look in the boxes on top, and they find canned peas, so they don't bother looking in the boxes on the bottom, and they don't see all the dynamite. Got it? We get stopped and they see a rabbi, they're gonna look in every goddamn box we got."

The boxes in the back of the Toyota contained about a quarter of the supplies that Cowboy had been able to deliver to them. There was going to be a good use for it after all. That thought alleviated some of Marty's distress. He loved blowing things up. And now that they knew there was something worthy of his skills, well, maybe it wasn't such a horrible thing to have to put on the clothes of a priest to get that opportunity. But he sure as hell still wished it didn't have to be something that had a skirt on it!

Right after Rosie and Tsali had returned from the mountains with news of the rebel camp, the call had come in from Beeker. Beeker said, "This one's important, guys. Do what you can till I get there. I'm on my way."

According to Rosie, there was a whole army out there. Not a little group of banditos, not some rabble-rousers. There was a goddamn army.

There were only the five of them and Tsali. Actually only

three of them and the kid right now. Cowboy and Billy Leaps still hadn't arrived. Somehow the odds had to be equalized. Rosie had estimated a camp of three hundred men—they had no idea how large a portion of the total troop strength that represented. But that wasn't the issue. That group was large enough that it would help a lot in the future if they could be neutralized.

Tanks. Mortars, Rosie had seen lots of mortars. Hundreds of enemy troops. There must be an ammo dump. There should be some fuel held in supply to power the tanks. Just calculating an inventory of potential destruction made Applebaum feel better.

Ammo dumps and fuel storage tanks would make his own explosions even more spectacular. If he could just figure out . . .

"We're getting close." Harry smiled and made a quick sign of the Cross to some small children staring at the passing truck from the side of the road.

"I'm all set," said Applebaum. "I'm ready for action. Everything's ready to go. Everything'll go great if I don't trip on these fucking skirts."

"Okay, Marty, okay."

They purposely avoided the exact place on the map where Rosie had reported the camp to be. If they'd discovered the two dead sentries, their security was likely to have been doubled. Just the thought of those two dead men—and the boy who'd had to kill them—made Harry sad all over again, and the smile he'd kept since he'd prepared it for the children was erased.

Tsali had done the right thing. Beeker and Delilah seemed to expect the information they'd received over the telephone, but they were also grateful for the verification.

The papers and the clothing tags that Tsali had retrieved from the two sentries he'd silently killed confirmed a presence of equipment and arms from communist nations. The uniforms proved to be Polish. The belt buckle he'd slashed from one of the men had markings that suggested Czechoslovakia as its origin. The men's sidearms were Hungarian FEG model FPs. Whoever was out there had the full support of the Eastern Bloc.

Harry'd left the main road, and the Toyota took them even higher into the mountains, up toward an old group of small farms that had been abandoned several years back when a landslide had destroyed a full year's crops and the farmers who had planned to harvest it. If their reading of the map was right, there would be an opportunity just about . . . there.

Harry stopped the truck and turned off the ignition. They sat still for a few minutes, just listening with their heads out of the window.

Nothing.

"I'm going to look around," said Harry. "Don't start unloading."

Harry got out and walked east through the brush. The path was a steep downward slope, and he grabbed bushes to help make his descent slower.

Behind him, Marty had begun unloading.

The edge of the cliff came quicker than Harry had suspected. He stopped short, and a little flurry of rocks and clotted earth spilled over the edge. Harry held on tightly to a bush, knelt down, and peered over the edge.

There was a sheer drop of about a hundred fifty feet. Directly below was dense forest and a hundred yards beyond that was the clearing that Rosie had told them about.

It would have made strategic sense to put the camp right up against the face of the cliff—if the cliff had been stable—but there had been small break-offs and fairly recently too. When Harry looked straight down he could see bare earth below, evidence of a recent slide, but already it had begun to be covered with vegetation springing up.

It then occurred to Harry that it would also have made good strategic sense for the camp below to station sentries up on this plateau as well, if for no other reason than the vantage it provided of the rebel camp.

Suddenly Harry shivered within his cassock. He got quickly but carefully to his feet, turned right around, and hurried back to the truck.

His instinct had proved right.

There stood Marty at the open back of the truck, hands in the air, while a man in a brown and green uniform pointed an AK-47 rifle at him. A second guard was just about to open the first of the boxes that Applebaum had set out on the ground.

Harry stepped on a twig—probably the only dry twig within a radius of ten miles. The twig snapped, and the guard turned with his rifle, pointing it on a level with Harry's heart.

# 26

But the guard wasn't quick enough, because Harry already had his pistol out and had fired. Twice. Both bullets went through the sentry's head.

At the same time, Applebaum had kicked the guard who was kneeling before the boxes. Just once. Under the chin. Breaking his jaw and sending him backward, colliding with the guard Harry'd killed.

Harry dragged the bodies out of the way, tying and gagging the one who remained alive, then set about unloading the truck. Applebaum made his own investigation of the territory then. He was the professional now and didn't even seem to notice that he was still wearing the cassock.

In ten minutes he returned to the truck, knelt in the dirt, and began making scratches with a small stick. A condensed map of the plateau, with some calculations and *X*'s. That's all he needed.

He stood up.

"Let's get rid of these clothes."

Harry didn't argue. If they were found with the dynamite, the cassocks weren't going to be much of a disguise.

Someone watching would have been hard put to decide whether Marty had looked more ridiculous in his cassock than he did now in his underwear and boots, with a holstered pistol under his left arm.

Harry followed him about with a box of the dynamite under either arm, and Marty set the things up. For some of them Marty scooped out shallow depressions in the earth with his bare hands. For others he climbed into low trees and placed the charges of dynamite in the branches. Yet a third set of explosives were suspended from ropes against the face of the cliff, about fifteen meters down.

None of it made sense to Harry, but he asked no questions. What would he have done with the answers anyway? He already trusted Marty completely.

The whole business took an hour and a half. Harry's thick body hair was plastered to his torso. He could smell himself. That used to embarrass him when he was a young boy, how strong his odor was. Now, after years in Vietnam and more years in a barroom on the South Side of Chicago, Harry wasn't sure he'd know what stink was.

No more sentries presented themselves to be killed, which both Harry and Marty considered a piece of luck. Half an hour more Marty occupied in checking what he'd done.

Harry had one more charge of dynamite, which he proffered to Marty.

Marty's brow furrowed. "I don't know what to do with it."

"Good measure?"

Marty placed the last charge on a small bush very near the edge of the cliff and attached the appropriate wires.

They returned to the Toyota, and Harry asked, "Are we safe here?"

Marty shook his head, and Harry drove the vehicle about

a quarter of a mile farther away from the edge of the cliff as Marty fiddled with the small switchboard on his lap. It was the size of a computer keyboard.

Harry stopped the Toyota and glanced at his friend. "What are we waiting for?"

"I sort of wanted to watch," Marty said.

"Not a good idea," said Harry, but Marty already knew that. So with a sigh of resignation, Applebaum flipped five of twelve switches and then began to count aloud.

"One. Two. Three. Four. Five . . ."

Maybe it was that Marty had the instincts of a geologist. He had a cousin who was a geologist and made lots of money working for one of the oil companies. Maybe it was just that he had done this sort of thing before. Maybe he was instinctual, or plain lucky.

Whatever the reason, his plan worked.

The first five charges, those suspended against the face of the cliff, detonated all at once, blowing out rock and dust and spilling it over the camp. All the rebel soldiers stopped what they were doing and stared up at the cliff that loomed over them. It seemed very close all at once.

Then five more explosions occurred, these sending up five geysers of dirt and vegetation at the top of the cliff, out of the line of sight of the camp.

Then there was a pause, but in the pause came a rumble and a cracking, and as the rebel soldiers watched below, with horrified fascination, a slice of the cliff, shaped like a wedge of lemon, came loose at the top and began sliding directly toward the armed camp.

Some of the soldiers began to run, away from the cliff, into the forest. Most just stood and watched, unable to move or to comprehend their own terror.

The wedge of earth, weighing no more than a couple of hundred thousand tons, slipped slowly free of the top of the cliff. If it had fallen straight down it would have landed in the forest between the camp clearing at the base of the cliff, but it didn't quite do that. It flipped over once, quite slowly it seemed, so that the men looking up could see trees and bushes and dry grass on the still-whole surface of the wedge.

And as they looked up, those trees and bushes and dry grass exploded in terrible fire and noise as the third set of Applebaum's explosions was triggered. The wedge, in the air above the camp, broke apart, and a third of a million tons of debris rained down on the Communist encampment.

It was no more. All of it obliterated.

Then, as if to add insult to injury—or merely to take care of those fortunate enough to have escaped major injury by fleeing into the forest—the earth shook again, and explosion succeeded explosion beneath that new mound of earth.

*Boooommmmm. Boooooommmmmm. Bo-boo-boooommmm.*

Throaty and muffled.

Some of the burning trees had fallen on the camp's fuel supplies. And the earth that had poured down on the camp a few moments before was now shot back high into the air, and burning gasoline spewed out over the forest.

Those who hadn't been crushed to death now died a death that was slower and more painful.

Marty, in his underwear, sat in the front seat of the Toyota with the board on his lap.

"I hate it, I just hate it, Harry, when I don't get to watch."

"We ought to check it out."

"You think I didn't do it right?"

"I didn't say that." Harry started up the truck, and they

went slowly down the road. At the turn-off, they'd go directly for the camp. If Marty'd done his work properly, there wouldn't be much in the way of resistance to their advance.

"I did it right all right," Marty murmured, depressed. "Probably one of my great jobs. My really great jobs. I hate it when I don't get to watch."

There was no one to stop them, but before they got anywhere near the camp, they were assaulted with the stink of burning gasoline.

"See," said Marty, "it was a fabulous plan. I got the fuel supply too. I mean, I am one smart son of a bitch."

He was one smart and very depressed son of a bitch.

Harry got out of the truck and scanned the area with field glasses.

In a moment, he called Marty out of the truck.

"Marty," he said, handing over the glasses, "look over there at the face of the cliff."

Marty took off his own glasses, wiped his eyes—still watering with pollen—wiped his own glasses, and then at last raised the binoculars. He peered through them at the cliff face.

"Goddamn," he whispered, "smooth as silk. Look at that. And every-goddamn-body who saw it is dead."

"No," said Harry, "look under that."

Marty trained the glasses lower on the face of the cliff. The explosions had shaken the side of the plateau with the force of an earthquake. More than just that wedge of earth had come loose. All the vegetation that had crawled up the face of the cliff had been shaken loose, as was the detritus of centuries of earthslides.

And what that did was to reveal something that hadn't been seen for five or six hundred years.

A wall of carved blocks.

Marty put down the field glasses and looked at Harry.

Harry shrugged. "Some kind of temple, I guess."

"Goddamn," whispered Marty in a brightening tone. "If I ever have to give up blowing off people's heads, I'm gonna become a goddamn archaeologist. Wouldn't Mama like that!"

# 27

The couple who got out of the cab in front of the Hacienda Taninul did not look like the perfectly average American married couple.

For one thing, she was beautiful. So beautiful that men looked at her and assumed two things. One, that she was dumb, and two, that all women should be that dumb. Her hair was blonde and golden in a way that could have upset the gold market in Zurich. Her breasts would have provided an agnostic proof of a God in heaven. Her legs and the rest of her body gave the overall impression that she was the ultimate, final, and optimal result of four and a half billion years of cellular evolution.

She let her husband take care of the cab fare and the luggage while she looked around the plaza. Her smile, if she smiled in hell, would have compensated the damned for damnation.

Her husband scowled. Her husband was obviously uncomfortable in his expensive sports jacket. The tightly wound muscles of his chest were apparent, for his sports shirt was open to the solar plexus. He'd made no attempt to hide the disfigurement of a torn and mangled ear. And, in general, the way he moved and looked about him suggested that luxury hotels in the capital cities of the world were not his favored place of residence.

No, not exactly the normal American couple who visited San Sebastian.

The woman handled business inside the hotel, for she spoke Spanish, and he evidently did not.

She didn't have to speak Spanish. The staff of the hotel would have thrown themselves off the roof for her smile.

She signed the registration card *Mr. and Mrs. W. L. Beeker* and gave their address as *Shreveport, Louisiana, USA*.

Mr. W. L. Beeker handed over a corporate credit card, but the clerk had never heard of the company he represented.

The bellboy took them up to Room 465, and Delilah smiled and tipped him. As soon as he'd left, Beeker opened the door and knocked at the room directly across the hall.

Tsali opened the door to his father.

For one moment, Beeker threw his arms around his son and hugged him close. Tsali hugged back. Then the moment was gone, and Beeker once more was the leader of the Black Berets. He strode into the room, saying, "All right. Full report."

Rosie lay on the bed. Marty and Harry sat at the table near the windows overlooking the plaza, playing cards. None of them jumped up in welcome.

"We got it all, Billy Leaps," Rosie finally spoke. "We got too much."

"They got Russian backing, like we told you," said Harry. "Marty took out at least four T-sixty-twos—"

"And about three hundred men," added Applebaum soberly.

Beeker exchanged glances with Delilah, who'd just come in: What was going on here? Marty Applebaum had taken out a force of men, including major armaments, and he wasn't yelling and screaming, jumping on the bed, and tearing down the curtains?

He looked at his three men, then at Tsali. The boy seemed downcast as well.

It was Harry who spoke.

"Beak, after Marty and I took that camp out, we rode further up in the hills. Didn't come across any more camps, but it was obvious—they got all kinds of troops out there in the mountains. There's Indians up there, and those Indians have been terrorized. Usual stuff: Taking out the men, raping the women, and shooting the kids so they wouldn't run off and report troop movements."

"Yeah," said Marty glumly—even he was affected by what they'd seen—"usual stuff."

"Beeker," said Rosie. "We can't give you an estimate, but I'll tell you one thing. If they were able to get T-sixty-twos in here, there's not a damn thing that's beyond them. That, and we just don't know how many camps they could have up there. I found the one, and Marty took it out, but after that—"

"Yeah," said Beeker. "I know. Trouble."

# 28

The bitch had damn well better have found him a decent helicopter, that's all Cowboy had to say about the matter. Get him out of Louisiana and make him leave the fucking ranch undefended, make him desert Sambo's sister and what that sweet cripple could provide him. Well, he had to admit, Delilah had done it good. It wasn't just a decent helicopter.

It was a Hughes AH-64, one of the best the U.S. had in operation. How Delilah had gotten it to San Sebastian, Cowboy didn't know. He did know it had arrived in the belly of a C-130, a transport plane that was big and bruiser enough to carry around such things. But from where? There were no markings on this baby. No U.S. Army, no nothing. Virgin as a saint. Only pure camouflage paint on it.

No markings on the C-130 either. There were American troops playing what seemed to be perpetual war games in Honduras. Could have been from there. Did Delilah have those connections? Or was it something even more? Was there some force so powerful and rich that it had its own arsenal of AH-64s and C-130s?

Cowboy didn't care. He just knew he had the copter. It was in mint shape, so new he suspected it hadn't been flown on anything but trial missions before. The big, powerful machine made him feel pretty good. More than pretty good—it was wonderful. He always felt that good when he was in the air. But this bird made it even better than usual.

There was the power of the two 1,536 hp General Electric engines, for one thing. That, and the complex "Black Hole" system that miraculously worked to cool the engine exhaust so quickly that heat-seeking missiles were stymied for a target. They'd have to get him with regular arms.

And if they tried that, he had his own to fight back with. There were 16 Hellfire missiles on the four wing hardpoints. A 30-mm Chain Gun on the turret under the fuselage ready with 1,200 rounds of ammunition. This wasn't going to be any easy baby to knock off. No way.

Cowboy scanned the land beneath him. They had to know how many more of the enemy existed. There had to be more than the one camp Rosie had spotted and Marty had taken out. But without a better idea of what they were up against, they couldn't possibly plan sufficiently for the battle they now were convinced was going to come.

The copter was moving at an easy cruising speed of 150 miles an hour. Cowboy was looking for a major encampment. The one they had discovered earlier hadn't been covered or hidden. It had been large enough for the four tanks. There was every reason to suspect that the others would be similar operations.

Cowboy's surveillance map had been sectioned off to give him a clear view of how he was going to work. One area at a time. Tanks, he reminded himself, he was looking for tanks. Large groups of troops. And just about anything else on the ground that wasn't an Indian hut. Except the Russians could hide in Indian huts just about as well as anything else. He was looking for *anything*, and he had to trust his instinct to tell him what things were dangerous.

He found something dangerous, all right. It wasn't troops and it wasn't tanks, and it wasn't even on the ground.

It rose up in front of him without warning, and in such a maneuver that Cowboy knew he had provided every bit as much of a surprise to the other guy. The other guy, he knew immediately, was an M1-24, a "Hind-E." The Soviet machine that was the major Russian entry in the copter stand-off in Europe.

The computer in Cowboy's brain rang off the data: the Hind-E was an armed gunship. It had four barrel cannon with air-to-air and air-to-ground capability. A powerful 12.7-mm gun right at the nose was aimed right at Cowboy this moment, as the two startled pilots stared at one another through the tiers of smoked glass. The Hind-E had four 32-round racks of missiles in the rocket pods, and the bastard carried four 551-pound bombs in its belly.

It wasn't an untried machine either. This was what the Russians were using in Afghanistan. It was battle-tried and true. A machine to be contended with, one that you didn't take for granted.

Cowboy instantly went into a battle mode. But before he had a chance to move against the Hind-E, it was moving away at top speed. His AH-64 should be minimally faster. He could catch up with it. But he held back. The Hind-E obviously had a mission. Better to find out what it was than to just take it out.

There was something else. Something that bugged Cowboy. The two machines had hovered in the air facing one another for maybe five seconds before both veered away. In those five seconds, the lone pilots stared at one another. And the other man was familiar to Cowboy. Cowboy had seen this guy before. Somewhere. *Where?*

The other man had flipped Cowboy the bird! He'd recognized Cowboy too, and he'd given him the finger. Then he flew away fast. So who the hell . . .

*Jack Seeley.*

In Texas. Jack Seeley was the man who'd been an overseer for the crazy right-wing bastard who'd captured Cowboy and added him to the chain gang that was digging irrigation ditches on his property. Seeley was an overseer, with a bull-whip.

But it was Seeley who'd saved Cowboy's life. Thrown him candy bars for strength. Helped the Black Berets in their assault on the stronghold. Flown the copter that they'd come in on.

And afterward something had come between Seeley and Billy Leaps Beeker. Cowboy didn't know what, and Billy Leaps wasn't telling.

Now Seeley was in San Sebastian flying a Communist helicopter and the Black Berets were there waiting for a Communist revolution. What the hell was going on?

Cowboy decided that the information that Seeley was there was more important than anything else he could discover for the guys today. He turned his machine back toward Huasteca. There was some deep shit going on, and the rest of them had better be clued into it. Right now!

# 29

It wasn't the way Tsali had wanted it to be.

His feet were sore, terribly sore. He knew that no matter what he did he couldn't sustain the trial of the half-marathon. His feet wouldn't take it. But there was still the 8,000-meter race.

It would have been a wonderful opportunity. There was his father in the stands, looking down at him. It should have been impossible to pick this one man out of a crowd of twenty-six thousand, but Tsali's eyes had gone right to him. This should have been his moment. He had wanted to prove himself, to make himself a star in front of his father. He'd dreamed about Delilah coming up to him after he'd won the gold medal and kissing him. Then his father would have come up, shaken his hand, man to man.

He winced as the pain in the sole of his right foot shot up his leg. He was going to have to will the pain to go away. He could not give into it. Not in front of his father.

Strange. Twenty-six thousand people. Tsali had never seen so many people gathered together in one place. If he'd thought about it before, he would have imagined that he'd be frightened, performing before an audience. Displaying whatever weaknesses he had before a crowd of onlookers who would not necessarily be sympathetic to him. Losing before twenty-six thousand people. Twenty-six thousand people privy to his personal humiliation.

But he didn't care about those twenty-six thousand. They might as well have been the cardboard cutouts of humans that his father nailed to trees for target practice. Tsali cared only that his father was watching.

Earlier that day Rosie had taken him out of the half-marathon. In the locker room afterward, Maka Sefa looked at the revised list, with Tsali's name crossed off, looked at Tsali, and smirked.

Rosie said, "I'm sorry, kid, but you can't do it. I may be a fake coach, but I'm still your coach, and I say no."

Rosie didn't offer any consolation beyond that, and that wasn't much. But his unspoken addendum was: This is an assignment.

The opening ceremonies that morning had lasted two hours, and most of the speeches had been in Spanish. Tsali was surprised just how much of the speeches he was able to understand, even after so little time in the country. But a boy who cannot speak does a great deal of careful listening. *Part of the assignment.*

There'd been some field events, two women's races, several men's dashes, and now the 8,000-meter race. It would have been better for Tsali's chances if the race had been scheduled later, but for the Black Berets, this time was optimal. They suspected that something was going to occur this first day of the games. And Tsali, even as he was on the course, had been given his job to do.

Tsali, Maka Sefa, and half a dozen others crouched at their marks.

*Crack!*

Tsali took off.

He imagined himself one of his ancestors running freely

through the American wilderness in a loincloth. He took the pain in his feet and he willed it to be the determination of the Cherokee.

Ten thousand meters is a distance just over six miles. Rosie had wanted Tsali to remove himself from this list as well. Now that all the Black Berets were in San Sebastian and the games had begun, they didn't need to maintain the cover so rigidly. A disappointed runner was just as good a disguise as a winning runner, anyway. But Tsali had refused, and in that refusal he came as close as he ever had to being violently willful against one of the Black Berets.

As the pain began to mount in his lungs, becoming one with the pain in his feet, he remembered that this was his own choice. His one time for glory. He had picked it. It was his own decision.

Around the first lap they went. The runners were grouped tightly together, no one making a move yet. In a race of this distance you had to maintain a pace that would not exhaust you immediately. Ten thousand meters might not be a marathon, but it had its own rhythms. You had to run with strategy and thought, and not just the pumping of your legs.

As they began the second lap Tsali glanced up at Billy Leaps in the stands. *This is for my father.*

It was also for the Black Berets.

They wanted him on the track, and it really had only been concern for his feet that made Rosie advise him to drop out.

Rosie hadn't argued much when Tsali refused.

They wanted Tsali to watch the stands and see if anything was out of place. He had been trained to observe. From the track itself, Tsali would obtain an overall picture of the stadium that the others, in the stands, could not.

He knew that the team was spread out in the seats. Delilah sat in the presidential box, and there would have been very few who suspected that the beautiful American seated behind President Salazar was also acting as his bodyguard.

Rosie was in a trainer's stand near the track. Beside him, hidden in a pile of running gear, was one of the Spanish machine guns they'd smuggled in. It was loaded, ready for action. Marty and Harry were wandering the stands at the other end of the arena. They, too, had the powerful guns hidden in bags.

They were only a few men, one woman, and a boy on the track whose legs and lungs were vying for a gold medal in pain. But they were ready to take on an army. If only they knew what the army was. Tsali wanted to give them the answer. He was finishing the third lap of the race. Maka Sefa was beside him. The young black man looked over and grinned cruelly at Tsali, as if to say, So sorry, little Indian boy, you're not going to make it.

Tsali's mind overruled his emotions. His nearly every impulse was to spurt forward, leaving Maka in the rear. But he would have been foolish to give into that. He wanted to win. He wanted that gold medal. His coolness seemed to bother Maka. The black boy looked angry—it was amazing how much you actually *could* see, even in the blood mist of such exertion. Suddenly it was the African youth who moved forward.

*Fool.*

The pain subsided a little. With Maka's waste of precious stored energy, Tsali could see the chance to gain his own victory. He would allow the African to have the fleeting glory of the lead. He would be more cautious, smarter, just as Rosie had told him to be.

The fourth lap of the race brought no change. Maka held a small lead. Behind Tsali was a Somali boy who kept pace with them in third. The others trailed behind. Tsali's eyes kept racing over the stands. *There is great danger here.* Where was it? He was approaching the presidential box again. Delilah was standing, clapping her hands. Delilah wasn't the sort for raucous cheering. In front of her was the good man his father had saved. And by the time all that had registered, Tsali was past them.

Now he'd think about the race again, give that a precious second of thought. He'd—

Then Tsali saw the Slav.

Dmitri Blyushkin.

He would never know what established that first connection in his mind. Somehow his thoughts about Rosie's having a machine gun in his trainer's area was part of it. There was also the slightest out-of-sync move on Blyushkin's part. The big man—a Bulgarian, Tsali remembered—was moving in a way that he ought not to move.

Tsali wasn't sure what he meant by that, but that something was wrong was apparent to him.

Maka Sefa's Bulgarian trainer was moving away from his seat. He was carrying a large towel draped loosely over his right arm, concealing his hand—and whatever was in it. It looked ordinary enough for a trainer to be carrying a towel, but there was a combination of things: the way his arm was hefted, the fact that he was moving away from the track, his inattention to the race in which his protégé was running, his concentration on something that was in the direction of the presidential box.

*I want the gold medal!*

But Tsali knew that it wasn't going to be his. Instinct rules the warrior. His father had told him that. Trust your instinct. Now it told him that Blyushkin was an enemy and one who was going to strike in a matter of moments. They had tried to get President Salazar in Washington. Now an enemy was moving toward the president again.

By the time that Tsali had figured all this out, he was nearly a hundred yards beyond the presidential box, well on his way around the track again.

He put on a burst of incredible speed—all the speed he could muster.

He passed Maka Sefa in an instant. The black youth's face snapped right in surprise as Tsali went by, and in another moment, he'd put on speed too.

The crowd cheered, then broke off the cheer. This wasn't time for Tsali to put on his greatest speed. There were laps to go, before he gave his all.

And it was apparent that Tsali was giving his all.

Around the track with Maka Sefa at his heels.

Tsali praying to the god of the Cherokee that he would not be too late.

He was not.

Dmitri Blyushkin, taking advantage of the crowd's attention on Tsali, had hurried along the side of the track and was just about to mount the steps that would bring him close to the presidential box.

Maka Sefa pounded on the track behind the Cherokee boy.

In a move that no one in the entire stadium anticipated—not even Delilah, so close, or Beeker, watching his son from across the way through field glasses—Tsali veered off the track entirely. Without lessening any of his speed, and conserving all his momentum, he dived—head first—at the back of the huge Slav.

Tsali's hands were stretched in front of him. His first contact was with Blyushkin's throat. They grasped it round and did not let go, not even when the Bulgarian slammed against the concrete steps he'd been just about to go up.

All around the crowd gasped and screamed.

Down on the track, the runners faltered and slowed, but after a few moments picked up again and continued the race—though their concentration was broken.

Blyushkin struggled, but Tsali's hands held on his throat. The Indian boy's muscles had been stretched and strengthened on the Louisiana farm.

The Slav fired the gun that he had carried hidden beneath the towel, but it sent a bullet into the leg of a woman sitting nearby.

That set up a new round of shouts and near hysteria around them.

Tsali held on.

*I have lost the gold medal.*

His hands were the outlet for all his frustration and anger. It flowed down from his brain and heart, through his arms, and strengthened his fingers around Blyushkin's neck. He didn't even feel the arms that tore at his, trying to loosen his deathly grip. Tears of disappointment flowed down his cheeks as Tsali strangled all the breath and life from the Bulgarian assassin.

# 30

The moment Tsali left the track, Beeker stood up, his SIG revolver in his hand. He trusted the kid to give a signal only if it was truly necessary.

So Beeker was convinced that something was happening.

The sight of the American tourist with a gun in his hand caused an immediate panic around him. His neighbors rose and tried to move away, but they succeeded only into knocking one another down and blocking Beeker's way out.

Beeker stood on his seat and looked around. Something was happening at the president's box, only a few hundred feet away. The crowd blocked his view. He did see Rosie, however, pulling Tsali off the man he'd jumped.

In another part of the stadium, another commotion showed itself, and at the center of that were Marty and Harry, who leaped down onto the field and took a short cut across to the president's box.

Of the six runners on the track, only Maka Sefa was still running, but when the black athlete glanced into the stands and saw that it was *his* coach whom the American Indian boy had attacked, he stopped in amazement and horror.

Spectators were leaving the stands as quickly as possible, some of them onto the field, others attempting to leave by exits that were already stoppered with frightened people.

Amid all this tumult Beeker saw some pattern emerging.

The pattern was easy to make out, because it involved the athletes in uniform.

A number of them swarmed onto the field, with faces set and purpose in their steps. They conferred briefly and then split up, some of them going toward the exits and others toward the presidential box. Their calculated movements were in stark contrast to the panic in the crowd.

That panic was shocked into silence by the noise and physical reverberation of several explosions crowding in on one another.

*BAAM! BAAAAM! BAAA-BAAAAA-BAAAAAAM-MMMM!*

All heads turned in the direction of the noise. Flames and black smoke appeared over the rim of the bowl.

The airport, Beeker realized.

After that single moment of shocked silence, the entire stadium erupted in frantic movement and noise. The crowd's movements now made the previous moment of panic seem like a fire drill in a parochial school.

Fury boiled in Beeker's blood as he raised his glasses and scanned the area near the presidential box, looking for Tsali, Rosie, and Delilah. He could only catch glimpses of what was happening there.

What was happening was that half a dozen of the uniformed athletes had lifted President Salazar and were carrying him out on their shoulders, pushing their way toward one of the exits.

The president was struggling, but he was no match for these

well-trained youths—and to those around, it looked merely as if the athletes were trying to remove him from the danger.

Beeker had to get there!

He shot his revolver into the air to encourage movement in the crowd of civilians that hemmed him in.

The shot only made the crowd scream and tear at his legs.

It was just possible that Billy Leaps would be torn apart by these people if they conceived that he was the cause—and not the cure—of the danger in which they found themselves.

As he stood on the seat with his pistol raised in the air, he looked about him. Hundreds of people, dark-skinned, dark-eyed, staring at him with fear and hate in their eyes.

He made a lightning-quick decision. He was about fifteen feet from the railing at the lower end of the stand. The edge of the field was about ten feet below that.

Billy Leaps took the only route that was available to him.

He walked across the crowd.

Placing his right foot on the shoulder of a man who stood directly in front of him, he took a long stride and placed his left foot on the head of a slightly shorter man.

The two men dipped under the weight and the push of Beeker's feet, but the Cherokee was so quick that he was to the railing before any other of these human stepping-stones had a chance to get out of the way. He may have broken a shoulder or two behind him, but he was at the rail. He stood poised there on the slippery aluminum for a second, and then he performed a perfect flip down onto the earth. The flip wasn't for show. It gave him an easier landing, with much less pressure on his legs.

He raced across the floor of the stadium.

Just in time to see six more athletes disappear through the exit.

With an unconscious Delilah on their shoulders.

The revolution had begun.

An hour later the group was gathered in the hotel room—the whole group but Delilah. Rosie was sitting in a corner with Tsali. The kid's stoic expression didn't fool anyone. He was in great physical and psychological pain. Not only had he lost the race, he'd abandoned his discipline and attacked Blyushkin not so much with skill or strength, but with blind fury.

He'd lost control.

Beeker knew the boy needed something from him, but this wasn't the time to worry about bucking up the offspring.

Cowboy had been waiting for them, with his report on Seeley.

Somehow, Billy Leaps wasn't surprised.

Seeley had warned him, in that dreary bar in Texas, that the next time they encountered one another, they'd be on opposite sides.

Beeker knew the story—none of the others did.

Jack Seeley had been a green pilot in Vietnam. He was flying a copter that was supposed to retrieve a squad of marines who were under attack. Beeker had been in the craft with him when Seeley decided that the mission was too dangerous. He refused to land the chopper and pick up the men. He was scared to die. Beeker made him more frightened. Beeker put a gun to the pilot's temple and advised him to land.

Seeley had pulled off the mission, even won a medal for it. He won the medal and tasted glory and pride and the whole business that makes men heroes. What's more, he went on with it—got women, and publicity, the infatuation with danger, and the belief that death doesn't come to the man who is unfalteringly brave.

Years later, Seeley had a chance to return Billy Leaps's favor by helping to rescue Cowboy. The debt was discharged. But then Seeley warned Beeker that when next they met, Seeley would have another thing to pay Beeker for—the hell he'd been consigned to, the minus side of being a hero, the obsession and the fascination with danger, the knowledge that he'd die a miserable, lonely, and painful death, the impossibility of his ever establishing a normal life.

He had Billy Leaps Beeker to thank for all that too.

A man out for that kind of vengeance was more dangerous than the total of his fighting skills. Seeley knew he'd die in battle—he wouldn't have the usual allotment of human fear to make him sane and careful and rational. Now or next week. This day or next year. It didn't matter. When the time came, Seeley would give up his life for that speck of vengeance.

He had the skill to pay Beeker back. They'd all seen it. The way he'd flown their mission in Texas proved just how good he was. He could do a fair amount of damage, that was certain. Especially at the controls of a copter as powerful as the Hind-E.

If there had been any question about that, what he'd done at the airport cinched it.

The surprise air attack had destroyed San Sebastian's tiny air force along with every commercial plane in the country. Seeley's bombs and missiles had been used with unerring care. He had worked so quickly and effectively that the small contingent of the San Sebastian army stationed at the airport hadn't been able to get off a dozen rounds at him before he'd veered off, complete destruction in his wake.

The destruction of the airport had also acted as the signal for the Communist plants at the games.

The trainers and athletes from the Eastern Bloc countries had transformed themselves into a professional—and very military—team the moment Seeley's explosions had sounded. They'd left the stadium and destroyed all communication between Huasteca and the outside world.

The enemy had eliminated any hope for immediate requests of outside aid. Their forces were on the move. The small San Sebastian army had reports of two more columns of armor approaching the city. There had, in fact, been two more groups of armor in the hills besides the one that Applebaum had taken out. The enemy also had control of the air.

Except for one pilot with one helicopter.

"You got to take Seeley out," Beeker announced to Cowboy.

"Done." Cowboy, as always, was wearing his dark glasses with the mirrored shades. It was impossible to see his eyes.

"And I'll find Delilah," said Beeker.

Neither statement was bravado, but each carried the unspoken addendum: *I'll do it, or die trying.*

The Black Berets were moving.

# 31

The city was quiet, almost dead, outside the windows of the Hacienda Taninul. Inside the room occupied by the Black Berets, there was no noise either. Five small suitcases had been opened and the contents spread out on the floor and the bed.

Camouflage pants, jungle boots, black shirts, and cans of grease to be applied to one another's face.

These were men who rarely touched one another, even in the easy communion of a single household. But now there was no hesitation of hand against face, neck, and shoulders, as they smeared one another with the black paint.

It was the first time that Tsali had cammied up. He stood quietly before his father, as Billy Leaps Beeker's roughened hands smeared the black paint over his son's visage.

Even Marty Applebaum was silent as he dressed. It was as if his raucous personality had been thrown away, and nothing was left of him but that part which was totally Black Beret.

When each man was done, he turned away from the others, faced the wall and his own thoughts. Checked his gear. Prepared for death.

Finally all that was left was Roosevelt Boone, his skin now no blacker than the others. He knelt in the center of the room, his head bowed. In his outstretched hand, he held a straight razor.

Cowboy and Beeker glanced at one another, and then both men at Harry.

Who would do it?

Beeker came forward. The leader, following a team ritual, would shave Rosie's head.

The black man had dampened his short tight curly hair with hot water, but there was no more lubricant than that.

The noise of the straight razor as it scraped around Rosie's massive head was loud, sharp, regular.

It took a full five minutes, during which time no one said a word.

Cowboy and Tsali stood at the window, looking out over the silent city.

Applebaum and the Greek sat next to one another in the room's two chairs, silent, unmoving, reading one another's thoughts.

*Scrape. Scrape. Scrape.*

When he was done, Beeker smeared the shorn head with a dullness of black paint.

Rosie, having communed with whatever African god lodged in his soul, rose up again a warrior.

Marty had been studying the map as he sat in the back of Cowboy's helicopter. He was flying with Cowboy to see which bridge was his most likely target.

Cowboy followed the route that the rumored easternmost column was bound to take. In a two-mile stretch of the road, about two hours in front of the advancing brigade, three bridges crossed a meandering sullen stream.

"I want that one," said Applebaum, as Cowboy flew over

the middle bridge. It was the longest, constructed of wood, reinforced with steel.

Not a big bridge—just two narrow lanes wide, just about forty yards long.

But it would do.

The meandering stream was shallow, with numerous sandbars. Cowboy set down on the largest, and almost immediately Harry and Rosie materialized out of the underbrush. They had stolen a jeep and made their way to this rendezvous point earlier.

In another moment Cowboy was wheeling up into the air again.

The other column was out there somewhere. He had to find it.

And he had to find Seeley.

Billy Leaps Beeker and Tsali had their own finding to do.

The streets of Huasteca were deserted. The terrified civilians had locked themselves away in their homes. San Sebastian had always been a peaceful country, one that didn't know the ravages of revolution and war that had torn apart so many of its near neighbors.

But television had at least suggested the reality of fighting and violence. The people of San Sebastian had seen Managua in flames and San Salvador in shambles. Maybe this too was to be their unlooked-for fate. They stayed inside their homes, or cowered in the churches, and prayed that whatever happened happened soon and was over quickly.

They hadn't learned the simple lesson that peace flies like the dove that represents it; war and destruction linger like an overfed sow, collapsed in the heat of its own wallowing.

Beeker and Tsali each carried one of the prized Amelis, with chest bands holding extra ammo. They moved along the blue-shadowed walls of the city streets, ducking into alleyways and recessed doorways, ready to fire.

Off in the distance—sometimes nearer, sometimes farther away—came the sirens of ambulances whining in the otherwise eerily silent city. Theirs was the song of sorrow that was sung in Beirut, Belfast, and Johannesburg, the chorus that followed in the track of the world's terrorists.

The two Cherokee had a goal. As they proceeded purposefully through the streets of Huasteca, Beeker took note of the highly developed skills that Tsali had developed. The seventeen-year-old moved with the unconscious grace and courage of the seasoned veteran. His face showed all concentration and determination, and not a whisker of panic or self-doubt. And this was the boy that the marines—God, even the army—would have turned away because he could not speak.

Not for the first time the father was overwhelmed with love for his son. His son who could stand beside him as his comrade.

The kidnapping terrorists had moved toward the eastern extremities of the city. Why? The Black Berets had asked themselves that question only once. To Tsali and Rosie, who knew the city almost as well as they knew Shreveport, the answer had been obvious.

At the eastern extremity of the city, in the richest suburb, was the Bulgarian Embassy.

An embassy was sacred territory. No American fighting unit would dare violate the diplomatic immunity that is accorded an embassy. It was a law of the international community that even rogue nations would adhere to. An assault on a sovereign embassy was an unthinkable action—and if the unthinkable occurred, as it had when the Iranians attacked the American embassy, then the whole world rose up in protest and denunciation.

An embassy was sacred territory—except to the Black Berets.

For the Black Berets, there was only justice. If justice dictated that an embassy be attacked and its inhabitants . . . *punished*, then that was what was going to happen. Despite what the arbiters of international law proclaimed in the Hague. Wherever the hell *that* was.

So far as Billy Leaps was concerned, the Bulgarian Embassy was a big white house with a wall around it. Inside the house were Communist criminals holding onto the man he had vowed to protect and the woman he . . .

The woman he wanted to save from danger.

The two Cherokee had reached their goal. The sirens were still singing in the streets of Huasteca. There was no longer any doubt that Billy Leaps and Tsali had found what they were looking for.

Fifty armed men stood guard before, and immediately behind, the entrance to the embassy grounds.

Through the locked and barred gates, Beeker could see armed vehicles in the paved courtyard.

The place was a fortress, and to take this fortress all Beeker had was himself, a seventeen-year-old boy with sore feet, and two untried weapons.

He'd do it.

# 32

Cowboy loved the big bird. He adored it. If he ever really did get married, he'd want it to be to something like the AH-64. That would be a honeymoon he'd never come down from. He didn't care if the machine was the most expensive helicopter ever built, he didn't care that there were certain regulations against civilian individuals owning top-of-the-line, state-of-the-art combat machinery, all he cared about was its performance—and that was beyond his power to praise it. Pure American technology and pure American know-how, all of it in this big, armored beauty of a helicopter.

They called the thing Apache. That was a shame. Think how much nicer it would be if it were the Cherokee—Tsali would like that.

Cowboy flew the bird so naturally that he could indulge himself with those thoughts as he scanned the San Sebastian landscape below him. It was dreary country—all green—supposed to be beautiful, but the sameness got to him. And reminded him too much of that other place. He wanted to see something different. He wanted to see metal monsters on the road, heading for Huasteca. He wanted to see metal monsters in the sights of the Hellfire missiles that this baby was nurturing under its stub wing hardpoints.

He was going to get his chance.

The column of armor came into view. It was going down the road as quickly as Cowboy had ever seen such lumbering vehicles advance—a pretty good clip. There was no indication of any resistance from the San Sebastian army. Its stores had been destroyed in the raid Seeley had pulled. If they had anything left, it was probably a box of tacks to throw in the path of the advancing tanks. Not much more than that. All their heavy arms had been gathered at the airfield. Probably some kind of mole had arranged for them to ignore the warnings that Delilah had delivered through the president. No one should be so stupid as to leave a whole army's weaponry in one place—even if that army was as small as San Sebastian's.

It was going to be up to Cowboy, and since Cowboy had said he'd take care of things, he figured he might as well get to work. Pleasant work. It was so pretty to see, little bobbing ducks in an arcade. That's all. A little target practice with a new air rifle.

His fingers were on the controls. The column had reached an area of cultivated fields, no more than an hour from the city.

They weren't looking out for air attack. They imagined that the air force of San Sebastian was burning on the airstrip outside of Huasteca. They were just speeding their way to the city, like college boys on their way to the first fraternity mixer of the season. Ripe for a little action.

Cowboy was going to turn that mixer into a hell week.

He was going to give these guys the ultimate hazing.

He waited patiently, hovering over trees to the northeast of the troops, until the last of the column came into view. Then he moved. He jerked the Apache forward top speed, never forgetting the careful calculations of distance and focus that he'd need. At the right moment, a moment so right it felt like a honeymoon ejaculation, Cowboy released the first Hellfire and watched the beauty of the missile's flight.

Goddamn, that thing *shone* in the sun.

*KE-KE-KE-BLAAAAAM.*

The tank erupted in a fury of fire and destruction. There was a quick afterexplosion—*BLAAAAM*—as the fuel caught fire.

The tank veered to the left, catching several troops beneath its massive treads, and a moment later Cowboy saw several more stick figures, burning, speed away from the exploded tank.

Poor bastards.

Cowboy hated to see suffering.

Rosie always said those men were chickens with their heads cut off. They didn't really feel anything. They were already dead. Dead as they'd be long after they'd toppled forward, and were still, and the flames had burned out.

Still, when you could see a man running around and everything from his boots to his hair was on fire, you couldn't help saying it to yourself.

Poor bastard.

The second tank was evidently manned by someone with decent training. He was trying to get Cowboy's Apache in his sights. Cowboy pushed a second button. Another Hellfire sped toward its target.

*KE-KE-KE-BLAA-KE-KE-BLAAAAAAAAAMMMM!*

Cowboy's aim was getting better. He got the fuel tank directly.

He didn't see it, because he was already on the other side and turning around again.

A halting swoop, just to stay out of anyone's line of fire, two more missiles, and two more tanks were down.

It had been a field of corn, nearly ripe for the first of the long growing season's two harvests.

Now it was burning sullenly, and the wrecks of the four tanks belched up black and oily smoke.

One more swoop, one more Hellfire missile, and the last of the tanks—just about to disappear beneath the cover of the forest—exploded.

The tank rolled into the line of trees at the edge of the field, knocked down a few trunks, set them on fire, and then expired in a rolling cloud of flames and heat.

Nothing left on the ground but a few vehicles on the road and a couple of hundred men who'd taken refuge in the burning cornfield. All of them who'd saved their weapons firing at Cowboy.

He tried out a few more pieces of the Apache's arsenal, targets having so conveniently presented themselves, mowed down a number of the Communists in the corn, exploded a few vehicles in the road, and even managed to pick off a single man he'd chosen at random.

When Cowboy saw this unlucky rebel cut apart with the bullets from his cannon, he banked the vehicle sharply right and headed off satisfied.

He still had to find Seeley.

# 33

There was a glint in Applebaum's eye. This was where he came into his own. This was when *he* was the leader and everybody else did what he told them to do. This was when he got to stand underneath the bridge, with Harry holding him around the waist to make sure the water didn't wash him away, and this was when Rosie was just lying up there on the planks of the bridge, handing down whatever Marty told him to hand down. And if Marty screamed, "Hey, fuck you, watch what you're doing!" they watched what they were doing. Because when it came to blowing things up, Marty was the boss.

Marty knew he had to do this one right, because up till now things hadn't been going right for them.

They were five guys, a kid, and a lady with big tits against an entire revolutionary army. The kid had sore feet, and the lady with big tits had been captured. The armaments of the San Sebastian army that might have helped them had either been blown to bits or were so distributed through the countryside that there'd be no finding them again.

In short, the odds looked bad.

And if Marty didn't do his job right, the odds were going to be worse.

"Just blow the goddamn bridge up," Harry suggested mildly. "My arms are getting tired."

"I don't just blow things up," said Marty. "I'm the Demolisher. I demolish things. You know who God is going to hire on Judgment Day? Martin Applebaum. I can do anything I want on earth, 'cause I'm getting into heaven on the Day of Judgment. Services rendered."

"In the meantime . . ." suggested Rosie from above, ready with Applebaum's wire.

"Yeah?"

"Blow up the goddamn bridge."

"Next piling," said Marty.

Harry waded with his friend across to the next set of bridge supports.

Rosie followed on the bridge above.

In half an hour, no one had passed on the bridge. The farmers in the area knew something was up. They weren't out for any early-afternoon strolls that day.

In the distance, a little while before, they'd heard explosions. No one said anything, but the three of them knew—Cowboy.

Nobody even bothered to say "Hope he's all right." Either he was all right, and he had won that part of the day for them, or else Cowboy was dead, and before this was over, they'd probably be dead too. So nobody said anything, when the echoing thunder of the explosions rattled over them.

Rosie was hot in the sun. It beat down on his back until his cammy uniform was soaked with perspiration. Beneath him the boards were hot.

They were also shaking.

"Shit," he said. "They're coming. Hurry up, asshole."

"Can't hurry art," said Marty quietly. "Wire."

Rosie handed down the wire.

Applebaum connected it, snipped it, checked it, and said, "Next piling, Harry."

The boards of the bridge were shaking more now, rattling the teeth in the black man's head.

"Oh, shit," he whispered, but he didn't try to hurry Applebaum. Because he knew Applebaum was hurrying. Doing it fast, but doing it right. Rosie peered down between the boards. There they were, those two weird friends, Harry standing massive in the swift current of the shallow stream, expressionless, stolid, holding up Applebaum, with a blackened face, blackened scalp and hair, and very stupid-looking horn-rimmed glasses attached to his head with a tight band of black elastic.

His nostrils were flared, and his eyes behind those thick lenses were wide—but except for these small signs, Marty Applebaum might have been changing a light bulb on the underside of the bridge.

"Oh, shit," Rosie said again. A jeep sprang over the crest of the hill, and right behind it came the first tank.

"Wire," said Applebaum.

"This is it," said Rosie warningly.

Applebaum took a deep breath, let it out slowly, and said at the very end of it, "All done."

Grasping the edge of the bridge, Rosie turned a little flip over and into the water.

Applebaum made one more snip with his wire cutters, stuck them into his pocket, and then hopped down from Harry's shoulders.

The jeep rumbled across the bridge.

The three Black Berets swam downstream, just beneath the surface of the muddy water.

Rosie didn't come up till he felt his lungs bursting. He turned to the left and hit the gravelly edge of a sandbar. He rose, sputtered, and scrambled into the thick brush that lined the edge of the stream just in case there were soldiers on the bridge, ready to fire.

There weren't. The convoy was lined up and halted just before the bridge—evidently there was some discussion of whether the bridge would hold beneath the weight of the tanks. The heaviest non-tank vehicle was brought forward and went carefully and slowly over the bridge.

It held.

The rebel soldiers cheered.

Some people will cheer anything.

Even looking for them, Rosie couldn't see any of the charges or wires that Applebaum had planted beneath the bridge.

He couldn't even see Applebaum or Harry. He prayed Marty was all right because it was Marty who knew how to pull the switches.

Seemed like an easy thing, setting off an explosion by remote control, but Rosie had learned that there was an art to it. And exact rhythm to every demolition job that assured maximum destruction. By God, Marty had that rhythm.

Right down in the core of his soul.

The first tank moved slowly onto the bridge, and though there were some creaking boards beneath it, the planking held.

The rebel soldiers cheered again.

When the first tank was halfway over, the second tank began its journey across. This would have been a mistake, of course, had this been a suspension bridge, but the distributed weight on this piling bridge actually made a collapse less likely. When the first vehicle had nearly reached the other side and the second tank had attained the middle, the third tank moved onto the bridge.

Goddamn, thought Rosie. These guys were playing right into Applebaum's hand.

On cue.

*BLAAAM!*

The planks directly in front of the first tank blew high into the sky. So did a couple of rebel soldiers. At least parts of a couple of rebel soldiers. Other parts just fell into the water. The tank either didn't possess power brakes, or else the driver didn't have the reflexes to apply them, but the vehicle simply pitched forward through the hole, with the muzzle of its turret plunging deep into the mud, before snapping off under the weight of the falling vehicle.

*BLOOOOMM!*

Equal charge, but directly beneath the second tank, so that the noise was muffled and deeper.

The tank dropped into the stream as if through a trapdoor.

*BLAAAM!*

The planks behind the third tank—as well as a jeep full of Communist-trained rebels—disintegrated into sharp splinters and hot nails, shards of bone and bits of flesh.

Two tanks had fallen into the stream. The third was caught between two gaping holes in the bridge.

There was a slight pause then, overlaid with the sound of shouting rebels and a fair amount of pointless gunfire—the rebels having no idea which way to aim their weapons.

The pause, Rosie knew, was for Applebaum to admire his handiwork from whatever place had him concealed.

Then on to Phase Two.

A series of smaller explosions.

**CRACK!** **CRACK!**

**CRACK!** **CRACK!**

**CRACK!**

The two outer pilings first.

Then the two inside that.

Then the piling in the center.

With just enough time in between the explosions to produce the pattern.

Rosie would have been more satisfied if Applebaum had just done his business, without worrying about the aesthetics of the job.

Though it was nice, he had to admit.

The third tank went into the water when the bridge beneath it collapsed.

The men in the water, thrown there by the earlier explosions or having dived in to help their comrades escape from the overturned tanks, were killed by the debris.

Already the stream was running red past Rosie.

Time to go back to work.

Rosie climbed up the bank and sneaked back to where they'd hidden their rifles.

There'd be survivors to pick off.

Harry and Marty were already there.

"Hot shit, huh?" Marty grinned.

Rosie didn't even answer. He didn't want to get Applebaum started. He knew he'd be hearing about all this for the next three months anyway.

Or at least until Applebaum blew up something else.

# 34

The Apache swept through the air, seeking its foe. This was the one. The thought ran through Cowboy's mind. There is always one of them out there, one of them who just might be as good as he was. He hadn't found that one often, though there were some in 'Nam that had come too damn close. But Seeley, Seeley was it, the worthy opponent.

He was somewhere in San Sebastian right now. The tanks weren't going to make it to the city. The word must have gotten back to Huasteca by now. Seeley was the only advantage the revolutionaries still had. The only one. He had to be there.

Cowboy headed back for the city. He'd used his missiles. There was only the 30-mm Hughes Chain Gun left. It would have to be enough.

Huasteca came into view. This whole damn country probably wasn't bigger than Maryland, and the Apache afforded just about Instant Anywhere.

No mistaking the signs of a city under siege. Streets that were preternaturally quiet and streets that were in flames. It was the saddest sight in the world, houses and shops burning without anyone trying to put out the fires. Even the owners of these buildings stayed away and wept in safety.

Over the noise of the blades Cowboy couldn't hear arms fire, but eventually he made out, in a rich suburban sector, several cadres of fighting men.

Corpses along the well-tended streets.

Cowboy veered away from this trouble, not wanting to risk even a chance shot against the Apache.

His quarry was in the air.

If the San Sebastian regular army was losing against the fake rebels, then it was Cowboy's job to play equalizer. If they were winning, Cowboy would help to quicken that victory.

He found evidence of a large explosion—he must have missed the missile itself by only moments.

The massive radio tower near the great government house slowly toppled to the west. It crashed into the city square, destroying a turn-of-the-century fountain—dedicated to the freedom-loving people of San Sebastian by friends of liberty in the United States of America.

A bomb that could do that must be coming from Seeley.

Cowboy steered the Apache that way. He could only hope that Seeley's raid had used up his own big stuff. He could only hope that they were going to have a fair match.

Cowboy's hopes soared as he approached the square, where the tower lay crumpled and sparking with live electricity.

The unmistakable outline of the Hind-E rose from behind the Capitol dome.

It was Seeley.

He was hovering now, obviously ready to turn and go back to his base, wherever that might be, and reload. He *thought* he was going to.

Cowboy had to do this right. This wasn't just a guy on the

other side, this was his worthy opponent. He had to do it honorably. He moved into range and stabilized the Apache, just waiting for Seeley to notice him. They were close enough that Cowboy could make out the man's features when the Hind-E turned.

It was amazing just how much you could see up here.

Seeley's head snapped back in one moment's surprise.

Then he nodded.

Accepting the terms of the challenge.

They were warriors with respect not so much for one another as for the concept of warriorhood. Their steeds were mechanized, Seeley was in the pay of the enemy, Cowboy was operating a machine that should never have been in his possession—but they were honorable jousters on that field of air over the central square of Huasteca.

Seeley suddenly sent the Hind-E rising fast above the Square.

Cowboy instinctively dived to the right.

The noise of the 12.7-mm four-barrel gun on the Hind-E sounded above the chopper blades, and out of the corner of his eye Cowboy caught a glimpse of their flash.

But he and the Apache were no longer in their path. The bullets rained down on a confectioner's store and a stationery shop.

Cowboy raced in a downward spiral now to find his own spot from which to attack. It would have to be fancy. It would have to be fast. It would have to be perfect.

Cowboy didn't want to defeat Seeley with anything less than perfection, that was all.

He found his opening quickly, much more quickly than he had even dared hope. Seeley had been momentarily blinded by a sudden change of wind that blew smoke from the burning tower against the Hind-E. When he passed out from that screen of oily blackness, desperately maneuvering to get the Apache in his sights again, Cowboy's fingers were already on the lever to loosen the cannon.

He pulled the lever and the cannon burst open.

There was a moment—a tiny sliver of a moment—in which Cowboy relished his victory and marveled at the speed of this joust.

Then Cowboy was pulling straight back.

And ahead of him, the Hind-E was performing the crazy movements of a wounded bird, jerking and jumping the way a man does when he's been hit. The rotors looked as if they were about to stall.

Cowboy fired once more, even as he was traveling backward. The second round of cannon fire found the fuel tank.

The Hind-E exploded over the central square.

Seeley would not even have had time to think *I'm dead.* And there wouldn't be enough left of him to collect.

Cowboy pulled away without a backward glance. The whole thing—from Seeley's acceptance of the challenge to Seeley's raining down over the streets of Huasteca—hadn't occupied more than forty-five seconds.

# 35

Billy Leaps and Tsali were lurking in an alleyway not fifty yards from the front entrance of the Bulgarian Embassy.

Entry that way was impossible. Fifty guards to block the entrance of just two men. Even if Tsali and Beeker managed to kill every one, there'd be others, alerted by the noise.

Beeker gestured, but the gesture was lost on Tsali.

He'd already gone ahead to fulfill the order that was only just forming in Beeker's mind.

The kid was getting ahead of him.

Tsali knew every back way in Huasteca. By a circuitous route of narrow alleys and shadowed lanes between high white walls with flowering vines spilling over, Tsali led his father to a blank wall that looked like every other.

Tsali nodded once. It was the wall of the Bulgarian Embassy.

Handing Billy Leaps the Ameli, the boy sprang onto the trunk of a tree that had split open the side of the street in this back way, shimmied up it, and scooted out along a branch.

He reached down for the two machine guns and then gave his father a hand up.

In another moment the two of them had dropped down into the shrubbery outside the kitchens of the embassy. The door to the inside was open, but all was quiet. Evidently the native staff had fled the place.

For a full minute, Tsali and his father waited silently, crouched in the flowering bushes, until their very sweat had dried and they smelled nothing but the riotous blooms around them.

No one had heard or seen them.

No guards came this way.

Beeker looked at his son. Together they rose, hurtled the distance to the wall of the embassy, and crept along it till they were near a set of French windows that opened into one of the principal reception rooms.

All the while Beeker was plotting strategy. How was he to use this minimal force of two men against an enormously more powerful and plentiful enemy? Surprise was his only advantage.

Surprise and the Amelis.

Inside the room, through the open door, he could hear the conversation of two masculine voices, in Bulgarian. He remembered the language from Delilah's interrogation.

Carefully, with the assurance that Tsali was sweeping this small side courtyard with the machine gun, Beeker suddenly spun around and planted himself in the open doorway.

All his careful calculations splintered apart.

He froze.

Delilah was there. Bound tightly to an upholstered chair.

In front of her a Bulgarian, still wearing the uniform of one of the athletic coaches.

There were three other Bulgarians in the room, one at the desk on the telephone, two more conferring in the corner over a map.

Salazar was there too, tied to another chair. But there was a difference in his captivity. The president of San Sebastian still had his clothes on.

Delilah was naked. Her legs were obscenely spread apart by the ropes that attached her ankles to the legs of the chair. There, in plain view, was that secret part of her that Billy Leaps had seen only in their most intimate moments, that part of her that he had loved with his cock, his hands, his famished lips.

The Bulgarian in the coaching outfit wasn't just looking at Delilah's ravishing body: His hand pawed at her. Despite her stoicism, Beeker could read a grimace of pain and disgust that fleetingly crossed her face.

It wasn't much to see—and maybe nobody but Billy Leaps would have seen it—but hurt, terrible hurt was waging its battle inside her.

"Fucking bastard, get away from her!" Beeker was already inside the door. The Ameli's bullets could have penetrated a steel helmet at a third of a mile.

But the Bulgarian was only ten feet away, and he wasn't wearing a steel helmet.

In one sweep Beeker got him and the man on the telephone.

The Bulgarians holding the map between them looked up in surprise, and Beeker's bullets perforated the map.

They also perforated the Bulgarians holding it.

"Tsali!"

The boy swung immediately into the room.

He stopped short, momentarily stunned by the sight of the nude and blood-spattered Delilah. Almost immediately, however, he regained his composure. He drew out a knife, went round the back of her chair, and slashed the ropes that bound her.

First came the fools.

The ones who simply burst into the room to see what all the noise was about.

They piled up for a little while inside the doorway, then for a few seconds there was silence and stillness, then Beeker fired the Ameli he had trained on the door.

Gunfire behind him.

He whipped around.

Tsali was blowing away three guards who appeared in the open French doors.

Glass shattered outward. Guards screamed, groaned, and pitched forward through what few panes remained intact.

"They'll be coming," said Delilah, who'd managed to untie the president.

Before other guards appeared outside, the four of them climbed over the pile of bodies in the doorway and went into the hall. Beeker first, to sweep the area; Tsali last, to guard their rear.

Beeker mounted the principal staircase of the embassy three steps at a time, and on the second floor kicked open door after door.

He found a single employee, a mild-looking male with an even milder-looking revolver pointed waveringly at Beeker. The mild-looking man got a line of holes across his belly.

The four went into what must have been the ambassador's bedroom. It looked out over the front courtyard. Peering cautiously out the window, Beeker learned why there had been so little response to the gunfire that must have been heard in the room below.

The rebel soldiers and Bulgarian guards were otherwise occupied.

A small contingent of San Sebastian regular army were sniping at the rebels and the Bulgarians from the safety of nearby buildings. Even as Beeker watched a Molotov cocktail sailed end over end through the air and exploded against one of the armored vehicles in the compound.

Two nearby rebels were sheeted in liquid flame.

Beeker used the frame of the Ameli to break out the glass of the windows in front of him. Then he stuck the barrel of the gun out and fired randomly, forcing the enemy troops to find cover from the rear assault as well.

Only then did he begin to aim the Ameli.

The machine sang in his head.

Bodies fell in the courtyard. Sometimes they jumped backward—which meant that Beeker had got them. Sometimes they jumped forward—which meant they'd been shot by a San Sebastian sniper. Sometimes the bodies did a little jerking upright dance—which meant they'd been hit simultaneously, before and behind.

The window next to Beeker's had already been open, and Tsali stood there. His son's Ameli joined and increased the chorus of death.

A man and his son fighting their enemies. It was life or death, but it was life or death together.

The guards had at last made out the source of the attack from the house. The AK-47s rattled in response. The *pings* of the bullets snapping against the stuccoed walls of the embassy came closer.

Suddenly there was a much nearer rattle—an AK-47 right behind him. Beeker knew that. He turned, stunned, ready to face his death. But the AK-47 wasn't aimed at Beeker. It was being fired out into the courtyard from the next window.

Still naked, still smeared with the blood and body debris of the massacred Bulgarian, Delilah stood at the window firing one of the Russian automatic rifles. Her stance and expression were unconcerned, as if all this were just a peculiar sort of wild party, where one came nude and fired guns out of the upstairs windows—and as if she had been to such parties before.

She probably had.

President Salazar had a smaller weapon and was guarding the door against intruders.

Tsali was now gone, Beeker noticed, but he trusted the boy. If he'd gone somewhere, he'd gone to someplace where he needed to be.

Beeker went back. A dozen of the Bulgarian guards remained. They were the pros. The ones who'd responded to the surprise attack quickly enough to obtain decent cover. Their bullets might find human targets.

Beeker aimed. Knowing this battle could be long, too long. Wondering if his ammunition would hold up. He was the one barricaded on the inside this time. He was the one who would have to stand against the blockade.

"Beak!" shouted Delilah. He drew back instantly, as did she, and a spray of bullets shot through both windows, digging two lines of holes in the ceiling.

He flipped around again, his Ameli aimed out the window. He saw the man who'd fired. He'd been crouched between an embassy limousine and the outside stucco wall. He was taking aim again, but if Beeker could—

Beeker didn't have to.

The man's body suddenly rattled and danced behind the cover of the car, and his face suddenly gushed blood.

Tsali.

He'd crept downstairs and outside. Taken his deadly aim at the Bulgarians from behind their defenses.

The boy began spraying the courtyard from the side.

The pros were getting it. Either from Tsali, or from Beeker and Delilah above, or from the snipers outside the walls.

And no foolishness on the boy's part either. When they were all dead, Tsali simply melted away back into the house. One moment he was firing from behind the cover of a blooming orange oleander. Next moment there was no more firing, and there was Tsali, standing in the doorway of the ambassador's bedroom, unable to suppress a smile of triumph.

Naked and filthy as she was, Delilah rushed across the room and hugged him.

# 36

The dinner was the best that San Sebastian had to offer, which was very good indeed. But besides the Black Berets and Delilah, only President Salazar was present.

The medals and decorations were the highest that the country had to bestow. But they were bestowed on the Black Berets in secret, only showed to the men at the dinner table and then taken away "to be preserved in perpetuity."

The only decoration they'd be allowed to carry back with them was a special citation for Martin Applebaum, for the discovery of an important Olmec temple. He was declared a friend of the San Sebastian Archaeological Society forever. Excavation of the structure that Marty had inadvertently uncovered in the destruction of the rebel camp would begin within the year.

Three days after the aborted revolution, the Russians, the Bulgarians, and the Cubans were gone.

Nobody had even realized that the Cubans had been involved in the operation. But now they were gone.

The destruction of the Bulgarian Embassy—it caught on

fire eventually—was blamed on an inexperienced cook who didn't know how to handle gas properly.

The people of San Sebastian were not to discover that it was five American men, a beautiful blond woman, and a seventeen-year-old boy who had saved their country and their democracy.

That was all right for the Black Berets. They didn't work for glory.

They didn't care that they wouldn't now be set up as gods in a country they'd probably never return to. To be revered—and probably resented—in perpetuity.

It wouldn't have been a good thing to have the real business known in the United States either. Congress took a dim view of any meddling it didn't initiate itself.

The Black Berets didn't care, because they'd gotten what they wanted.

Cowboy'd gotten to fly a new machine. He liked that. He'd jousted with an equal, and won. He didn't like having killed Seeley, but there was a satisfaction in knowing the thing had been done right.

Marty'd gotten to blow up a bridge in a very artistic manner and destroy an entire convoy of communist troops. Coming on top of the redhead in Vegas, this had turned out to be a couple of weeks to file away in memory's top drawer, for easy reference.

Harry'd gotten a chance to lose himself for a while, to occupy his mind and his body with fighting and strategy. He'd forgotten, for the length of the time he'd spent in San Sebastian, that he was a very unhappy man. The interesting thing about fighting for survival was that it left you the impression that there was something worth surviving for.

Tsali had gotten a gold medal—not for running around in a circle faster than seven other seventeen-year-olds, but for something a little more important. He'd saved the life of the president of San Sebastian, one of the bastions of democracy in the Western Hemisphere.

And finally, Billy Leaps. Delilah had already handed over to him the deed for the two hundred acres of land that would connect his two properties. With a little ingenuity, he'd be able to set up a path on which three or four laps would equal a marathon's twenty-six miles.

That made him, for one moment, feel foolish and selfish—that he'd thrown the team into action for *that*. He was glad that mission had been successful. He was glad for Salazar's sake, and San Sebastian's sake, and even for Delilah's sake.

But those two hundred acres—that wasn't what Beeker had really gotten out of the mission. He'd wouldn't have missed this opportunity for the world.

He'd been able to fight alongside his son. And now that it was over, he realized something else—something that hadn't been clear to him in the midst of the business. He trusted Tsali completely. As completely as he trusted the others. That made William Leaps Beeker a very proud father.

The day after the quiet dinner in the presidential palace, the Black Berets returned to Louisiana. Delilah, looking a little weary, saw them off at the airport. She'd take a later flight to Miami, and then on up to Washington.

Possibly she had a report to make to her superior.

Whoever that was.

Only Tsali bothered looking out the window as the plane veered out over the Gulf of Mexico. He watched the coastline of San Sebastian recede in blue haze.

A single day of revolution in this country that had known only peace for seventy years would soon seem like only a thrashing nightmare, dispelled and forgotten in the morning.